I0621974

A WOMAN
OF POWER AND INFLUENCE

Herleva de Falaise

II

First published 2020
Mifair Publishing – Potters Bar, Herts, England
Copyright: Michael Fairley

ISBN 978-0-9543967-5-6

Typeset in Times New Roman 13pt on 16pt
Design by Concept Design
Printed in England by Kindle Direct Publishing, an Amazon.com company

Herleva de Falaise

IV

Bringing history to life

A WOMAN
OF POWER AND INFLUENCE

Herleva de Falaise
From commoner to mother of a king

Michael Fairley

Herleva de Falaise

Preface

Although few know the name of Herleva
de Falaise outside of the world of historical
research, she was nevertheless one of the most
important women of the Middle Ages and had
a major impact on the history and events of the
11th century and, indirectly, on the next one
thousand years of French, English and wider
European history. Indeed, was probably one
of the most influential and powerful women in
much of the history of northwestern Europe.

Born in Normandy, France, in 1012 she became
the mistress of Duke Robert I at the age of just 16
and mother of an illegitimate son and daughter
by him. A son who was subsequently crowned
Conqueror and King of England – in turn bringing
almost 300 years of Norman rule and the French
language to the country.

Married to a Count – and one of the Duke's
closest friends – after her beloved Duke was
forbidden by the church to marry her, she had five
more daughters and three further sons, one of whom
became an outstanding military leader, a bishop and
an Earl, the other a key army figurehead and Count.
Both were key to the successful invasion of England
in 1066. Together, these three sons of Herleva were
to become the wealthiest and most powerful men
in England. Their uncle and cousins also played an

influential role in, first, the Conquest and then the development of Norman England.

This book sets out to present in a fictionalized way an account of the life, loves, children and historical events surrounding – and following – Herleva de Falaise, and her sons, William, Odo and Robert. All dates, names, places and events have been obtained through historical research and are believed to be substantially correct, although even research records show quite wide variations in some of the dates, names and events recorded.

Hopefully readers will find the story that unfolds to be an interesting and important historical insight into the life and times of a relatively unknown tanner and fur trader's daughter from Falaise in France, whose impact on the long-term history and evolution of England and France has previously been very little known and largely undocumented.

A woman of power and influence

Map of Normandy

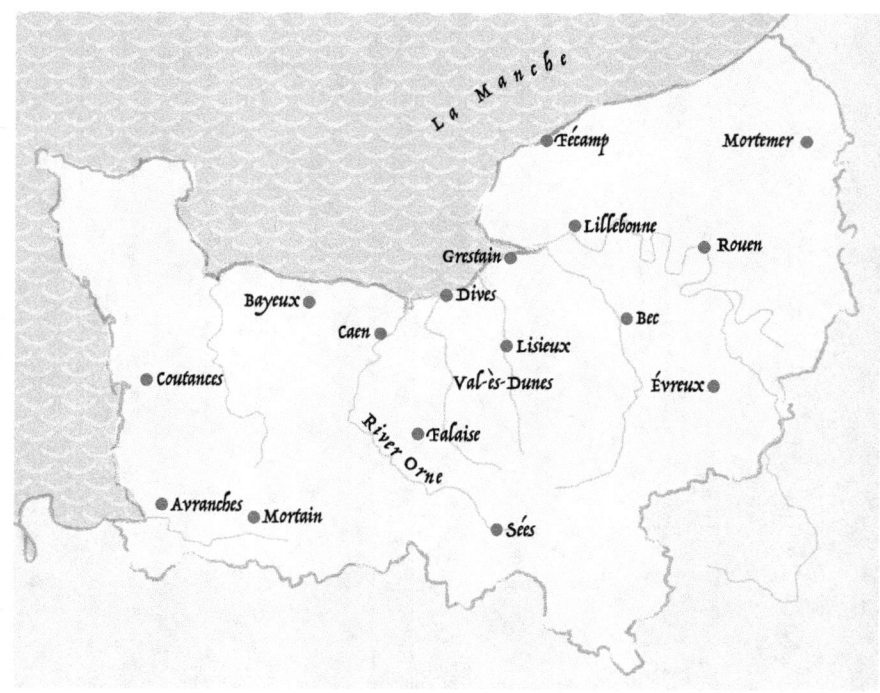

Map of Normandy region showing the location of the main places described in the book.

Chapter I

1027

It was early afternoon on a clear, and still quite warm, day in mid September and Robert, the young Duke of Normandy, had been looking out over the castle battlements for probably more than fifteen or twenty minutes. It was one of his usual mid-day after dinner haunts, largely because he never ceased to be fascinated by the impressive and breathtaking views that were set out before him. Today, with the sun shining strongly, it seemed even more impressive.

Below him when he looked through the embrasure – one of the openings in the battlements – were the shear walls of the castle, falling away in turn over a quite dramatic cliff face, rocky spur and promontory which plunged way, way, down below to the two valleys of the rivers Ante and Masceron, and the town, shops, businesses and houses of Falaise – a fairly small but quite prosperous agricultural and trading settlement of close to 4,000 people built-up around the castle and the surrounding area. The town and the many people who were working, riding, walking, pulling carts below - as well as children scampering around like little ants - all seemed to look so small from this great height.

Spreading out from the town as he looked over the battlements were the rolling hills, trees and meadows of the River Ante valley which further on flowed into the larger Dives river and, largely unseen from where he stood, the further valleys of the rivers Orne and Laizon which virtually surrounded the area. The Eraine hills lay far to the northeast. Some 30 or so kilometers to the north of the castle was the town and River Orne port of Caen, the largest city – and the capital – of Lower Normandy, and 13 kilometers beyond that to the north-northeast, discharging in to the Channel that could be crossed to England.

It was still difficult for him to believe that almost everything that he could see, from the castle itself to the surrounding estates, either belonged to him or paid rent to him – and that he was responsible for the security and safety of the Duchy of Normandy (the lands of the norsemen), the main towns and cities, the peasant villages and the people that lived and worked them. This was a Duchy created little more than 100 years previously when an agreement was drawn up between the King of France and Viking chief Rollo, and which now included many norse settlers and traders.

With little more than a year having passed since

his father Richard II, Duke of Normandy, had died
in his favourite residence of Fécamp castle and,
more recently, the death of his elder brother Duke
Richard III (in somewhat mysterious circumstances
that some believed his brother had been involved
in), Robert, now 19, still had senior advisers –
particularly his father's brother, also called Robert,
who was Archbishop of Rouen and the Count of
Évereux – to guide and help him to fulfill his duties
as the new Duke, yet he increasingly felt confident
in his own ability and powers.

As the head of the Duchy, it was his duty to
manage, feed, protect and clothe not just the family
members in the castle, but many relatives, fellow
men-at-arms – including well over 100 soldiers
– his chamberlain and family, many clerks, several
chaplains, workmen, and all the various marshals,
grooms, cooks, maids and other servants that a large
castle household required. He was the figurehead
of this vast court, with the diverse and spread-out
Duchy estates also needing to be managed, justice
upheld, guests to entertain and the, fragile as it
currently was, peace in northern France upheld.

In the hour between breakfast and dinner (which
usually lasted from around 11 a.m. to 12.30
pm), Robert had been reading court and Duchy
documents, signing and applying seals to others, and
listening to the thoughts and views of his uncle and
other advisers. Later, he would be continuing with
his ongoing lessons in swordsmanship, archery and

riding a horse into battle – all regularly practiced in competitions and jousting tournaments. Not that he believed he needed them any more. In his mind he was already better than most of his tutors. Indeed he would frequently be able to beat them in the many contests that he attended.

Turning away from the battlements Robert made his way down the long, often dark, stone stairways to the courtyard where the marshal in charge of the stables had already asked the Duke's groom to saddle and prepare his favorite horse – a sturdy white mare – ready for an afternoon ride out into the surrounding countryside. All around there was noise and activity. The clang of iron being worked in the foundry, coopers making barrels, armourers fashioning swords, and all kinds of other dedicated craftsmen at work, as well as young children at play.

Mounting, he rode purposely out through the main gatehouse entrance to the castle and down the long and at times fairly steep hill, on through the city gates and walls before turning away from the town, gradually moving from a slow canter into a more steady gallop, sometimes close to the river bank and at others through meadows or along cart tracks. Riding steadily for a near 20 minutes he slowly pulled on the reins to bring the horse back to a slow walk.

Ahead were a group of trees and just beyond them, he knew, was a slow-running and fairly shallow stream where it would be possible for the horse to drink and rest before returning to the castle. Moving into the shadows of the trees he dismounted and was about to walk forward when the sound of a voice talking or singing could be heard, followed by water splashing.

Intrigued, Robert stood quietly trying to assess the direction of these sounds and then, not more than several hundred yards away, he could see something moving about in the stream, finally recognizing this as the head of someone floating or swimming in the water. Were they in need of assistance? Should he go to their rescue?

Peering through the branches and greenery he was suddenly transfixed by the sight of a young girl standing up and walking towards the bank. Completely unclothed, the girl was an unbelievable vision to the young Robert, causing him to take a large breath. He had seen an unclothed female before, but nothing quite like this one. He was enchanted by her beauty and apparent ease in standing there without any worry on the grassy bank – but what should he do? If he made himself known she would undoubtedly be frightened away. He didn't want that. What he did want was to meet and talk to her. Who was she? Where did she come from?

Robert continued to watch from the trees as the girl, having stepped out of the stream and onto the bank, turned her back to him as she slowly used her dress to wipe some of the water from her body.

He hardly dared breath in case she saw him, and he could only hope that his horse, still quietly grazing, would also remain silent. Certainly the girl gave no indication that she knew he was there.

Slowly the girl dressed and then sat down on the bank, throwing pebbles into the stream and watching the ripples grow ever larger. All the time his heart was beating with the anticipation of meeting her. Finally, after some ten minutes he remounted his horse and slowly walked it forward to where she was still sitting and looking at the water.

Drawing close, the girl finally acknowledged his presence, jumping to her feet in apparent – perhaps even real – surprise. Robert looked at her face. It was even more beautiful than he had seen from a distance, with her long damp dark hair providing a natural frame to her large eyes and pretty mouth. Quite slim, she was somewhat shorter than him in height.

'Pray tell me your name' said Robert 'and where do you come from, for I do not believe that I have seen you before?'

'My name is Herleva de Falaise sire. I live with my parents in a large house by the river, close to yonder castle. You have probably ridden past it. The family trades in furs and leathers for the manufacture of all kinds of garments and their trimming, and we also have a workshop there that prepares the leather skins that will be made into the garments, as well as leatherware for the workmen and soldiers at the castle.'

'And your father's name?'

'Fulbert de Falaise sire. Perhaps you have heard of him. We have Viking ancestors that long ago settled in Normandy. His father is distantly related to the King of Sweden, while his grandmother was Queen of Norway, or maybe you know my uncle Walter de Falaise. He is a burgess of the town?'

'Yes. Walter I know well. Also Fulbert. He comes to the castle from time to time to tell us about various types of higher quality furs and leather for the craftsmen, although I didn't know that he had a Viking royal heritage. I should probably get to know him better. I believe I have spoken with him a few times. But let me dismount and take my horse to the water for refreshment before we talk further.'

Robert swung his leg over the saddle and stepped down onto the grass of the river bank, leading his horse to the water's edge where it immediately began to drink. He watched without speaking for a few minutes and then turned and walked back to the girl.

'May I sit and talk with you while the horse is resting'

'If you wish sire, but I must start my walk back to the town before long. I fear I walked far too much this morning and now have far to go to return to the town.'

Robert sat down on the bank, followed by the girl who, although not sitting too close to give him any encouragement, was close enough for him to once

7

again see and admire her pretty face. It was hard for
him not to stare at the girl, who seemed to him to be
so very young. Certainly looking much younger than
he was.

'Hold old are you?' he questioned. 'You look little
more than a girl.'

'I will soon be sixteen years of age sire, and
already a woman.' replied Herleva. 'I work with my
parents in the family business, helping to write and
keep records, and have done so for several years.'

'Then why are you not working today?'

'I come out into the countryside from time to time
to make a note of new sources of the bark and oak
galls that are used in the tanning of the hides. They
provide the tannins that are necessary for turning
them into quality leather. We always need new
supplies. But can I ask who you are, and what is
your name? Where do you come from?

'Just call me Robert. I live in the castle at Falaise.'
This obviously impressed Herleva from, first the
look, and then the attractive smile that crossed her
face, but she made no immediate comment.

Robert continued to gaze at the young girl,
wondering how he could meet and talk with her
again in the future - something he desperately
wanted to be able to do. He had already been
captivated by her charms, and she seemed bright,
intelligent and self-assured. Certainly there were few
in the castle or amongst those who visited who came
close to her looks. But how could a further meeting

be achieved? He must think of an answer.

'Now I must return to town' said Robert, rising to his feet as he talked. 'You said you were far from home. Would you care to ride with me?' At least he would be close to her for a while longer if she agreed. 'Why yes sire, but I will not come into the town with you. My father may get to hear and would not approve of me meeting with someone he did not know. You may leave me somewhere out of sight of the houses.'

Robert readily agreed. Mounting his horse he stretched out his arm. 'Please hold on to my arm mistress Herleva and I will raise you to sit behind me.' Effortlessly, he lifted her onto the rear of the horse, her legs both to one side. 'Put your arms around my waist and hold tight,' he said as he urged the horse forward.

Breaking into an easy canter they began their journey back towards the town, talking all the while. For Robert, the closeness of the girl behind him, with her body pressed up tight against his and her firm breasts touching his back, again filled him with a sense of excitement. He vowed to himself that he would find a way to meet her regularly.

As they continued to talk he learnt that Herleva had three brothers and a sister – Walter, Osbern, Reynald and Beatrice. Walter was a year older than Herleva, while Reynald was somewhat younger. Her sister Beatrice was the eldest and born four years before Walter. Her mother's name was Doda and she had been born in Scotland. Certainly a diverse and well-travelled family. They could be useful allies in the town.

Perhaps her brothers were a way of getting to talk with her in the coming weeks. She in turn learnt that he lived at the castle and was skilled in using a sword. She could already tell that he was a more than able horse rider and had an affinity with the animal - whispering words of encouragement or praise to the animal as they rode along. At no time did he let her know that he was actually Robert I, Duke of Normandy, fearing that this would turn her away from ever wishing to talk with him again.

From time to time he would reign in his horse, pointing out first a kestrel hovering above looking for food, then diving down fast to catch its prey, then a heron quietly fishing by the stream, a group of swans swimming by, rabbits scampering around. He was pleased that she was as interested as he in the nature and countryside of the region. Here was someone he enjoyed being with, and would like to spend more time with.

As they came closer to the town he came to a halt once again. 'Step down here mistress Herleva, and I will ride back to the castle alone.' Loosening her hold around his waist she slid to the ground, smoothing her dress and brushing the wisps of windswept hair away from her face.

'Thank you sire. I have enjoyed your company' she said, 'and thank you for bringing me back safely to town.'

'I will leave you now mistress Herleva. Hopefully we may meet again.' He waved a hand to her and kicking his heels to the horse's side began to ride away.

'I hope we also meet again' she replied, not knowing whether he had heard her call. She watched until he was out of sight within the town, never once looking back, before she started to walk the 500-600 yards back home, thinking all the time of the young man she had spent the last hour or so with. He really was quite handsome, strong, and very confident. They both had an interest in many things in common. Somebody that her parents could possibly accept if she ever managed to get closer to him?

Herleva de Falaise

Chapter II

1027

Later that same day, Robert was able to retire to his private chambers, which were managed for him from day-to-day by his chamberlain, and spend some time with other family members and key advisers, as well as servants and chambermaids to keep the chambers in order. This was a place for him to rest and have private meetings, as well as undertake leisure or entertainment activities with, for example, anything from playing board or dice games, watching jugglers, or listening to musicians, and local or travelling storytellers who told the fashionable tales of the time. It was also a place for private meals, mostly supper, at around four o'clock in the afternoon.

Finally, after eating and being entertained for a few hours, Robert was able to take care of his personal hygiene and wash. A bathtub was brought in and a variety of personal grooming implements were offered; everything from tooth picks, to combs and tweezers were provided. Once completed and everything cleared away he was ready to slip into his night attire and to retire to his bed.

Robert found it difficult to sleep that night. He kept thinking of the girl that he had met that day. Her nakedness in the stream. Her arms around his waist. Her bright conversation, and her pretty face and large eyes looking at him. He just could not forget her, His mind was thinking of all the possible ways of bringing her into his circle of friends.

It was well after midnight when an idea began to formulate in his mind. The more he thought about what he was conceiving in his half-asleep, half-awake state, the more it seemed feasible. Yes, tomorrow morning he would put his plan into action, he thought before falling into a deep and surprisingly restful sleep.

***

Next morning Robert was awake long before a guard in the castle keep sounded a wake-up call on his long hunting horn, which regularly happened each day shortly after sunrise. Time for everyone in the castle to rise but, before he did so, he once more turned his ideas of the night before around in his mind. Yes, this was a solution that could work. He would put it to his steward when they met for their daily discussions after morning mass.

Turning back the covers he rose from his bed.

Being September it was a somewhat damp and chilly start to the day so he partially dressed to keep warm before washing his hands and face from the wash basin in his room. Then, fully dressed he opened the door of his chamber to make his way to the hall for breakfast with his family and close friends.

Already the chambermaids were scurrying about and waiting to enter his chamber to take away any dirty clothing from the day before to be washed, empty the chamber pot and the dirty washing water, and air the blankets and furs on his bed. Walking through the stone-walled corridors some servants were still sweeping and tidying up from the previous evenings meal.

Morning breakfast was taken at a large wooden table with various family and friends that were in residence. Little more than some bread and a hot drink brought in by the servants, it would nevertheless sustain them until dinner was served in about four hours time. Conversation was usually about what one or another member had done the day before, or some local gossip that had been picked up from a servant or chambermaid, or what punishments were to be meted out.

Breakfast over, the group walked together to the chapel, meet the chaplain and participated in morning mass. This was normally celebrated every day without exception and was mandatory attendance for all those who were not away on some other business. Today the castle's small private chapel, which had painted walls and beautiful stained glass windows – an indication of the importance of the chapel to the family – was almost full. Religion was particularly close to the family, especially as Robert's uncle was Archbishop of Rouen, the most senior churchman in the Normandy region.

Mass was relatively short and, once over and having briefly discussed some planned future weddings, the Duke was ready to meet his officials – sometimes he did this as a group and at other times he liked to talk with them as individuals. Today, he had asked to talk with his steward and chamberlain first before any others. He could then sow the seeds of his plan to get Herleva into the castle and to have an excuse to see her every day. He was already convinced of the success of his idea.

Initially his discussions with them centered on all the normal daily and weekly castle and estate activities, which were often quite drawn out and onerous. Later, Robert began to turn the conversation quite naturally to his real purpose of the day.

'It is many months since I last invited Walter de Falaise, the burgess, to the castle to review progress in his ward. Would you both make the necessary arrangements for Walter to come to the castle next week to update me?' said the Duke. 'I also understand that he has a young son, William, as well as some nephews and nieces, the family of his brother Fulbert de Falaise. We could do with some new young blood to become squires, soldiers and ladies maids.

'Maybe one or more of these could be integrated into our band of trainee soldiers. The girls might be suitable for ongoing training as ladies in waiting or looking after visiting nobility. Perhaps you can ask the burgess to bring them with him, and then arrange for them to be shown around the castle and get a feel for its daily workings while I talk with him?'

'Yes sire, the chamberlain and myself will today place the necessary arrangements in hand and inform everyone that will need to be involved'. With that the two of them bowed and left the room.

So far, thought Robert, things are going as I had hoped – and nobody suspects what the real reason is for the meeting.

***

Time passed slowly for Robert during the week that followed, with the daylight hours until his planned meeting with Herleva's uncle giving him little time to either think about the girl or how she might be integrated into castle life. At night and alone in his chamber however, he had ample time. Each night was the same. Laying awake but with his eyes closed, thinking, dreaming, of when she would be coming to the castle. Of what she would say when she found out that he was the Duke, and how she would react when asked to live and work in the castle. And each night he would finally fall asleep - tired, anxious, but happy in the expectation that he would shortly see her again.

At last the day for the meeting with Walter de Falaise arrived. Robert awoke early and took more care than usual with his daily washing and dressing. He wanted to be at his best when Herleva came to the castle in case they should accidentally meet during her tour of the castle.

He took breakfast with the family and discussed with them the visit of Walter and his son, nephews and nieces, asking them to show the youngsters around, talk with them, and then let him know whether they might be suitable to bring into the castle for training. They all talked for some time about what they would like from the youngsters and promised to report back to Robert at breakfast the next day.

Prayers were taken in the chapel as usual, yet Robert found it difficult to concentrate. He was already thinking of what he might say when he eventually met Herleva again. How would she react on finding out he was the Duke? Perhaps she would feel he had deceived her by not telling her his full name when they had first met by the stream. Maybe she would not wish to talk to him.

***

By now, Herleva had been told by her father that

she would be going to the castle with her uncle Walter and that there was the possibility that she might be asked to live and work there to train as a lady in waiting or ladies maid. 'It would be quite an honor for the family and could be good for our business.' Fulbert explained to her. 'But how would you feel about it?'

Feeling that she was going a little flushed in the face, and not wishing to tell anyone that any chance of meeting the Robert that she had met by the stream and rode back to town with, would please her no end, she simply replied 'If that is what you wish father, I will do as you say.' Secretly, she could also feel her heart already beating a little faster, and already thinking of what she could wear so that she would stand out if he happened to spy her.

***

After chapel the following morning, Robert walked to his chamber and asked for his steward and chamberlain to join him. Castle and estate business took up more than an hour as they discussed work that needed to be undertaken on the castle and grounds, decided on punishments for tenants who were late with rent payment, reviewed the estate accounts and looked at requests for meetings with him. By which time it was announced that Walter de Falaise, the burgess, had arrived at the castle. Robert then asked the steward to go out and meet Walter, see that his son and nieces and nephews were looked after, and then bring him to the chamber.

'Good day Walter, its a while since we last talked. What's the latest news from the town? Robert listened intently while Walter discussed the latest developments, building work going on, trading conditions and the many people that were making their mark on daily life – both good and not so good. Decisions were made between them on matters that needed to be resolved. This all took at least an hour before the necessary town business was concluded.

'I believe you brought some of your children, nieces and nephews with you today Walter. I trust they enjoyed the visit? What did they think of the castle and the possibility of maybe working and living here one day? You did mention that to them before they came along with you? How was that received?'

'Generally with a great deal of excitement sire. It's a very hard life for youngsters in the town and the thought of being at the castle, learning new skills and trades, meeting new people and mixing with, and serving, some of the nobility created much discussion. They can't wait to one day meet with you.'

'In that case Walter, I'll leave it you to officially tell Fulbert's sons, who I believe are called Reynald, Osbern and also a Walter, that they are to join the castle and undergo military training. I believe we are all of similar ages, so I look forward to testing them with a sword one day. You can liaise with my steward and chamberlain about the necessary arrangements and introductions.

'Herleva, and possibly her sister, Beatrice, I'd like to consider becoming ladies in waiting or ladies maids to help in the many daily activities required to service my chamber, office and meeting rooms, and to look after visitors. Perhaps you can bring Herleva first. Come through the castle back gate one day soon. Let me know when so that I can be available to meet with her.'

***

Three days later, Walter de Falaise was back at the castle and asking to have a meeting with the Duke. By now, Robert had already received favorable feedback at breakfast from his family about bringing Walter and Fulbert's children into the castle, especially Herleva, who they thought was very pretty and bright. He therefore wondered what Walter might have to say, especially about Herleva. Could there be something wrong?

As he was shown into the room Robert spoke, perhaps somewhat impatiently. 'What is that you wish to speak with me about Walter?'

'I talked with Herleva, and her father, Fulbert, about her joining your service as a lady in waiting, but when I explained that she would be coming in through the castle back entrance with me, she refused. She says that she will only enter your service if she can come in through the main castle entrance in a way that will be an indication of her family's old Viking royal heritage and her future acceptance into castle life.'

Robert was at first taken aback. How could a Normandy commoner refuse an invitation to meet with a Duke and become a key part of the castle activities? It was unheard of.

'Take a seat Walter while I take a few moments to think what to do.'

Some ten minutes later, Robert came back to Walter. 'The girl shows great spirit and is very confident about herself. I've also heard her family does have some historical royal connections with the Vikings, which maybe could be useful to me. We need some new spirit in the castle women. I'm sure she will rapidly mark her mark. Let's humour her. I'll arrange for the stable to select one of the best white horses to go down into the town and let her ride on its back as she enters the castle entrance. The groom can lead the way, and I'll make sure that he also dresses in keeping with her entrance. Talk with her and her father, Fulbert, to arrange a suitable day and time then let me know. I want to be there to see this.'

***

It was a cold, but crisp and sunny day in mid December when Herleva de Falaise was led by a well-presented young groom into the castle on a large white horse. It had been specially selected by Duke Robert as the mare he had ridden the day they first met. He wondered if she would recognize it. For her part, she had dressed in the finest clothing that her father could afford, all trimmed with fur and leather from his shop. Even though she was not herself of Normandy noble birth, she was determined to show that she was someone that belonged in the new world she was about to inhabit.

Duke Robert, discretely out of her line of sight, watched with delight as she came through the main castle archway, under the latticed portcullis, and into the keep. Workmen, soldiers, servants, maids – all stopped to gaze on this beautiful, well dressed young girl riding confidently as she passed through them. She had certainly made her mark. Dismounting, she stood patiently waiting until a servant arrived to take her to meet the Duke.

The first part of his plan drawn up some several months before was working. He now looked forward to seeing her reaction when she came to his chamber, getting to know her and hopefully gaining her confidence so that they could be together. If possible, as his mistress.

Herleva de Falaise

Chapter III

1028

It was now early into the April following Herleva's introduction into castle life. There were a few signs outside that Spring had started to arrive, although it was still quite cold at night. Herleva had her own rooms in the extensive castle and grounds and a servant girl had been assigned to look after her. It was comfortable, and she was fitting in well with her duties, and also being further educated with other young ladies that had newly entered castle life.

With her knowledge and skills in leathers, furs and trimmings, Herleva had soon become popular with the noble ladies that either lived in or regularly visited the castle. They asked her advice about dressing smartly, she was able to help with creating or modifying good looking clothes for them – it was something she enjoyed, and she soon learned much of castle and duchy life from listening to the news and gossip amongst those she was mixing with on a daily life.

By now, she had found her way around most of the castle rooms and understood the many functionalities and activities gathered under its roof that were useful and essential to a Norman lord. Militarily training was always being undertaken each day, and the castle was certainly a well-defended refuge, with its windowless ground level and its thick walls, but also politically with its vast public great hall for court sessions and banquets.

Magnificent banquets would be held in the great hall on special occasions. Duke Robert, his family and important guests would sit at a high table, raised above other diners, and covered with a table cloth of fine linen.

On a daily basis, the castle could also accommodate the Duke's whole household inside its private quarters. The small private chapel enabled the residents to attend daily services without having to leave the building.

Herleva saw and talked with her brothers regularly when they came to the castle, and understood that they were already becoming quite widely regarded for their horse riding and skills with a sword, lance or bow, and were certainly enjoying their new role. Her elder brother Walter was of a similar age to the Duke, who seemed to like Walter's fiery Viking-like temperament, and undoubtedly got on well with the Duke – which pleased Herleva.

By this time, Herleva had settled in to quite a good life, and Duke Robert would now regularly come to see her when he was at the castle and sometimes ask her to stay the night with him in his chamber – which pleased her no end. He was away quite frequently, visiting relatives, seeing to the training of soldiers, overseeing Normandy estates, hunting and having meetings with the King in Paris, so there were often long gaps between their liaisons, which meant that when they did get together it would usually be with an urgency and passion in their love making, eventually both falling asleep tired, but very happy, in each others' arms.

At other times, when they were relaxing and talking together, she learnt that the Duke was having a number of problems with his uncle Robert the Dane, who was his father's brother and Archbishop of Rouen. While he performed a major role in the church and was an influential member of the clergy in Normandy, the Archbishop had also become heavily involved in Normandy political affairs and, as Robert's senior guardian, was trying to restrain his young nephew who had claimed the Duchy throne after his brother's death. As the most senior churchman in Normandy, he was certainly not in favor of the Duke having a mistress. Something he was actively trying to discourage.

From Herleva's periodic meetings and quiet chamber talks that would take place in between her amorous evenings and love making with Robert, it appeared that the Duke might be looking to take up battle with the Archbishop and was threatening

to banish him if he didn't stop interfering, in
which case he would also be looking to seize the
Archbishop's many properties.

She was in two minds about this: Her own family
was quite close knit and she couldn't image not
being able to meet and talk with them. Her uncle
Walter, the town Burgess, kept her informed of
town business, and her parents were always on
call if needed. Their guidance was important, even
if not always welcome. She therefore hoped that
Robert could reach accommodation with his uncle.
However, she also knew that the Archbishop was
trying to split her away from the Duke. Something
she desperately hoped would not happen now that
they had settled into a quite happy life together

It had been in mid January, less than a month after
her arrival at the castle that Robert had first told her
that he had fallen in love with her and wanted her to
be with him. By the end of that month she had been
convinced of his love (perhaps too easily) and they
had slept together for the first time, even though she
was by then only just 16. It was a passion between
them that she had never thought could be possible.
Indeed, something she never imagined would ever
have happen from that first day she had met the
Duke down by the stream.

Sadly, she also knew that it was unlikely that
they could ever be permanently together. She had
been a castle outsider and, although she had distant
Viking noble connections in the family, was not

really accepted as being part of the Norman nobility. They belonged to different social classes and marriage between Viking and Norman families was largely regarded as unacceptable, certainly by the Archbishop.

By now, it was undoubtedly common knowledge, at least amongst the main castle inhabitants, that the Duke had installed a mistress. This had happened a number of times before, but these did not usually last more than a few weeks, at most a month or two. It was a generally accepted practice of noblemen in France – probably worldwide – while they were looking for a suitable wife.

There was also no shortage of daughters of Norman noblemen that regularly came to the castle hoping to meet, and perhaps eventually, marry the handsome Duke. Not that she had seen any that impressed her too much. The problem was that they had powerful fathers who could easily – and often did – fall out with the Duke and make things difficult for him.

Neighbouring barons were already regularly waging private disputes and battles against one another. As such, a new, more powerful, aristocracy was starting to develop in Normandy. Herleva was already hearing from castle visitors that some members of the lesser nobility were already moving away from France to places such as Southern Italy – where an ever-growing Norman base was steadily building – and to other European regions, so as to seek better lives for themselves.

With all this in mind, Herleva had a somewhat fitful night. She was worried about the Duke returning from visiting his uncle in Rouen later that day and wanted to hear what they had said to each other. Was her relationship with the duke mentioned? She needed to talk to him urgently and knew that, depending on his discussions with the Archbishop, and news that had been given to her by her mother about Herleva probably being with baby, the end of their relationship might be close. Then what would happen to her?

Until a few days before, the thought of having a baby hadn't even occurred to her. She was still too young at little more than 16 years of age she thought.

However, this had all started to change the previous evening when she had spent time back at the family home with her mother, where she had mentioned to her that she had sometimes felt sick in the mornings and appeared to be putting on weight. After further discussion about changes in her body that Herleva had noticed she was experiencing, her mother, Doda, soon recognized that Herleva was almost certainly expecting a child. A child that could not be officially acknowledged, recognized or have any kind of title in life. Quite simply, within a few months Herleva would become the mother of a bastard child sired by Duke Robert I of Normandy.

Her mother spent some time explaining what

further changes would be taking place in Herleva's body during the pregnancy and the eventual birth, working out that this was likely to be towards the end of August or early September that year. Her father and brothers would need to be told. It had implications for all of them. 'More importantly,' said Doda, 'you are going to have to tell Duke Robert.'

'Will you please tell father?' Herleva asked her mother tearfully. 'I don't think I could face him at the moment. Do you think he will be angry?'

'I'll try and talk him around' she replied. 'You had better make your way back to the castle before it gets too dark. It will give you time to think how and when you can tell the Duke. Hopefully he will look after you and the baby.' With that, Herleva departed the family home, walking slowly back to the castle and deep in thought about her future.

***

It was late the following evening when the Duke sent his servant to bring her to his chambers. When she arrived he was sitting on some blankets and furs near a large open wood burning fire and looking somewhat distant.

'You look tired and exhausted sire' said Herleva. What ails you?'

'It's been a very long day, first the ride back from Rouen and then necessary discussions with the family and council. My uncle will not accept that his time as my guardian is finished and that I intend to make my own decisions. He has threatened to use force to take control − even excommunicate me from the church. I think I may end-up having to fight against him. But enough of my problems, I understand you wished to talk to me. Come and sit by my side. I need your companionship at this time.'

As she sat beside the Duke he leaned over and pulled her to his side, kissing her gently on the cheek as he did so, which helped her to relax a little − although still worried what his reaction would be to her news.

'I'm pleased that you could tell me about your uncle and your family problems. I hope it doesn't come to a battle. I couldn't bear it if I was to lose you. But I may lose you anyway when you hear what I have to say. Please do not be angry with me.'

The Duke looked alarmed at what she was saying. 'Why? What can possibly be so wrong? What can it be that is so terrible to tell me? I thought you were happy being with me at the castle. I certainly want you to be with me.'

'We have been together nearly four months now sire, and slept together many times when you have been at the castle. You have also looked after my brothers and found time to talk with my father. I couldn't have wished for more from you, and I hope you feel the same? But I have to tell you I am with child. My mother thinks you will be a father in possibly six months or so. I fear I will be sent away.'

At this time Herleva dropped her head and started to cry.

'Come close to me my love. I'm not angry with you. I really am pleased that we are expecting a new family member. I hope it can be a son. How this news will be treated by the family and council I don't know. Certainly the church, and particularly the Archbishop, will be displeased, but then he is displeased with me anyway. If I end up winning my feud with him he will be unable to object. Others may be a problem. It is too soon to judge. Hopefully we will eventually be accepted as being together and our child can be recognized as a rightful heir.'

'Thank you sire, I just hope I can be everything you want of me.'

'You already are,' said the Duke 'ever since I first saw you appear unclothed down by the stream on that day we first met, and you rode back into town with me.'

'You were there watching me, and didn't say anything!' she exclaimed with a laugh. 'Well, in that case you shall see me like that once again. 'With that she slowly slipped out of her dress and joined him on the bed, laughing, and relieved that he had accepted the news and overjoyed at being so happy. It was to be another evening of passionate love for the two of them.'

***

The next months that followed proved to be extremely difficult for both the Duke and Herleva. He was away from the castle more times than he was there, and she did not get to spend that much time in his company. He did send letters to her to update where he was and the problems he was facing, and also asking for news about the forthcoming baby.

Because he was absent so much and worried about how she might be being treated at the castle, the Duke asked one of his trusted noblemen – who also happened to be his best friend – Herluin, Viscount of Conteville, to regularly visit the castle and talk with her and reassure her that he was safe and would be returning.

Much the same age as Duke Robert, Herluin was a Viscount of rather moderate income and some land in the county of Mortain (Mortagne), where he had a small semi-fortified, chateau type, castle. Born in the Calvados department in northwestern France, about 22 kilometres from Falaise, he knew the Normandy region well, so could explain the Duke's travels – and battles – to Herleva. Over time she looked forward to his visits and updates. She missed the Duke not being there, missed having close male company, and undoubtedly flirted with Herluin when he was with her – much to his embarrassment.

The main news that Herleva received from both the Duke and from Herliun, was that the fall-out with Archbishop Robert had become even more serious, resulting in the Duke eventually attacking

34

the castle at Rouen and the Archbishop being sent into exile away from Normandy after refusing to accept the Duke's authority.

Even that was not the end of Duke Robert's problems in Normandy. The Bishop of Bayeux, Hugh d'Ivry, had become the next to question the Duke actions and his exiling of the Archbishop. The Bishop, who was senior among the Norman Bishops and located in a chapter that was one of the richest in France, was then placed under siege until he agreed to the authority and terms laid down by the Duke while, from exile, Archbishop Robert set about issuing a decree throughout Normandy banning the administration of the sacraments, effectively excommunicating his nephew.

***

It was not until close to the time that Herleva was due to give birth that Duke Robert was able to spend much time back at the castle with her. Herluin came to see her and the Duke quite frequently. They almost seemed like brothers at times and she had certainly grown quite fond of the Count.

Herleva and the Duke talked as much as they could during his consuming castle, court and other noble duties and she was often able to spend time in his bed chamber talking about what it would mean to the Duke to have a son. 'If we do have a boy, what name will he be called?' she queried.

'He will most definitely be a boy, and I thought we could perhaps call him William after your cousin. I don't think the nobles would let me call him after the family names of Richard or Robert. That would be too much for them to accept. He cannot be in line to inherit my title, but I would still hope we can give him a good life. He will need a senior figure in the castle to look out for him. I am therefore minded to make your father a chamberlain here when our son is born.'

***

So, at the end of August, 1028, a son was born to Robert I, Duke of Normandy, and Herleva de Falaise. His name was William. Additional maids and servants had been assigned to them, while her father, Fulbert de Falaise, had been appointed as a chamberlain to manage the affairs of Herleva and the young William, with responsibility for receiving and paying out money that the Duke had allocated for his son's upbringing.

For a while at least, everything seemed to be less stressful and more at peace with Herleva and baby William.

Chapter IV

1031

It was early summertime and it would soon be coming up towards three years since William had been born. Naturally inquisitive, even mischievous, he was already running around Herleva's chambers, or slipping out through an open door to hide in one or more of the corners and rooms of the castle. Servants and maids were frequently sent our to search for him and bring him back. Full of energy and much excitement he was undoubtedly a handful.

This was not helped as his father had spent considerable time being absent trying to quell disquiet and unrest breaking out in various regions of Normandy, and even beyond the region's borders into Flanders. Over the previous year Duke Robert had been called upon to provide both personal and military support to his neighbour in the northeast of France, Baldwin IV of Flanders. Driven out of his lands by his son, Baldwin had only managed to make peace with his son and return to Flanders with Duke Robert's help.

Flanders, which neighbours Normandy to its

southwestern border near the North Sea coast, was predominately flat and agriculturally fertile. It successfully traded in the weaving and selling of wool and cloth, and was one of the richest and most urbanized regions in Europe with its busy trading towns of Bruges and Ghent. It had therefore been important for Duke Robert to ensure that any unrest that arose close to his territories was kept to a minimum.

Herleva followed the Duke's travels and battles with much interest, worrying whether he might be killed or injured, or that Falaise itself might one day be invaded and overcome. Although largely supportive of the Duke's actions, she was necessarily concerned for herself and young William, but always reassured, by both the Duke and his friend Herluin.

It was later that same year that Robert was once again called upon to lend military support, this time to King Henry of France whose kingdom was under challenge from both his mother, and his younger brother. With the Duke's support, the King had eventually managed to retain his kingdom, granting land in northwestern France, north of the Seine toward Rouen, and known as The Vexin, to Robert in gratitude. It also helped protect the King from possible further invasions from the north.

Robert had additionally developed close ties with, and provided assistance to two English brothers, Edward and Alfred, his second cousins who were sons of Aethelred, King of England, and Robert's aunt Emma of Normandy, whose kingdom had been overthrown by Canute back in 1016. The brothers had already been living in exile with Robert at the Norman Court for quite some time, with the eventual hope or aim of taking back the English throne, hopefully with Robert's assistance.

Herleva had been able to meet and talk with them when they had visited the castle at Falaise and had therefore been able to get to known them quite well, enabling her to learn more about England, the English throne, Duke Robert's relatives in England and the country's ruling and political system – which seemed to be quite different to that in Normandy. She wondered how Robert might change that if he did one day become King of England.

To have the King of France, the, one-day, possible King of England, and Baldwin of Flanders as allies and supporters of both the Duke and of Normandy certainly pleased Herleva. Continuous years of battle and conflict was not what she wanted. What she did want was for the Duke to spend more time with her and his young son, William, in Falaise. Something that seemed to be increasingly impossible. More and more, she missed their time and intimacy together.

Although the Duke was away a great deal, he at least liked to play with William whenever he did return and could find the time. Herluin too, still visited frequently and was now treated more like an uncle by the young boy. Even Herleva looked forward to Herluin's visits; she had grown quite fond of him – even wondering what he might be like as a lover. Today he was expected to call with further news of the Duke, but she knew that nothing could possibly be able to happen between them.

What had also changed in the past months, and was making a big difference to Herleva's daily life, was that she and Duke Robert now also had a daughter, born towards the end of 1029 – a sister for young William, who he seemed to love playing with – who they had named as Adelaide. Adelaide de Falaise. She was by now already speaking, and looking to crawl or walk unsteadily around whenever she felt she was not being watched. Herleva expected that today Herluin was additionally coming today to see the young girl's progress and report back to the Duke on his mistress and children.

The other, and ongoing worry for her, was the continuing lack of acceptance of the Duke's authority by the church and many of the noblemen. Archbishop Robert was still in exile, now in Fécamp – a small fishing port on the Normandy coast in the Seine-Maritime department of the Normandy region – and from there making pronouncements about the Duke and church excommunication, while the Bishop of Bayeaux was still unhappy after being placed under siege and having to accede to the Duke.

For the past year, Alan III, Duke of Brittany and one of the Duke's cousins, had also become a problem, taking advantage of much of all the turmoil that had been taking place in Normandy and using that to try to break free of various policy controls laid down by the neighbouring region. This had led to Duke Robert attacking the region and then Alan retaliating. This raiding backwards and forwards between the two had already been continuing for quite some months, leading to Herleva seeing even less of the Duke.

Herleva's thoughts, which she often discussed with the Duke when he did find time to be at Falaise, was that this feud with the church and bishops needed to be brought to an end as soon as possible. Her liaison with the Duke as his mistress had elevated her from an outsider and commoner and she had undoubtedly acquired considerable power and influence – at least in the castle – through her relationship with him. However, as yet her views, although listened to, seemed to be generally un-headed by the Duke and the unhealthy feuding that he had with the church and barons still continued.

Indeed, at the present time she knew that he was overseeing the building of ships at various points along the Normandy coast, and that he was in the process of planning a possible invasion against the Duke of Brittany – who was continuing to make raids into places like Mont Saint-Michael, a fortified tidal island off northwest France which was in dispute between the two regions as to ownership. However, this time Duke Robert was looking to retaliate by invading by both land and from the sea.

How would that all end?

His continuing, but seemingly increasingly arms-length relationship with Herleva as his mistress through Herluin, and the fact that there were now two illegitimate children and no legitimate heir that could be accepted by the church and many of the senior hereditary nobles, didn't help either. The Duke's often expressed opinion to both her and Herluin was that 'I'm not going to be told by the church or nobles what I can and can't do in Normandy. I'll keep fighting until I have control.'

***

The Duke's continuing absences and Herleva's frustration at being left to raise the two children without him by her side was making their early and powerful love affair difficult to retain. Herleva increasingly felt that the Duke's feelings for her were being overruled by his continuing quest for control and power over all of his nobles, whilst there was also little support for her from within the church, who continued to rule that they couldn't be allowed to marry, and also that young William would never be allowed to inherit the title.

Would the Duke one day wish to marry someone of noble lineage who could give birth to a legitimate heir? It was often in the back of her mind, and perhaps Duke Robert's as well, but she felt it unwise to try and raise this with him.

However, the possibility of discussing all these problems and issues with Viscount Herluin when he came to visit was a great help and comfort. Knowing the Duke well, he at least had an understanding of where they were both coming from, but was nevertheless unable to interfere. Neither side would probably forgive him if he did, and he couldn't afford to fall out with either of them, especially Herleva, as by now, he too had also become enchanted by her.

***

It was few weeks later that Robert returned to the castle late in the afternoon. After eating, he retired to his chamber and asked his servant to attend. 'I would like you to deliver a message to mistress Herleva, and another to Viscount Conteville who is staying in the castle as my guest. Ask them both to join me at breakfast tomorrow morning and then for prayers in the chapel afterwards.'

'I will do that straight away sire. Sleep well, for you must be weary from your travels today.' With that he departed.

The following morning, the three of them had an early breakfast then went their separate ways to meet together at the castle chapel. Once prayers were over and they were ready to leave, the Duke bade them to accompany him to his private meeting room. 'I have a matter which I wish to discuss with you.'

Somewhat worried they followed behind.

Once seated, Duke Robert began talking. 'As you know, I have been troubled for some time by the attitude of both the church and many of the nobles to my role as Duke of Normandy. The Archbishop was made my guardian by my father, and he, as I think you well know, believes he should be the one making Normandy decisions, not myself. The Bishop of Bayeux has much of a similar view. I have already had to lay siege and defeat both of them. Both of them are still in exile, but this means that the church in Normandy is now almost paralysed. The Duke of Brittany is also claiming lands and causing unrest. This all has to be resolved if I wish to avoid permanent battles with various groups of warring bishops and nobles.

'Additionally, as you already know, the Bishops will not accept you, Herleva, as my mistress – or my wife – or William as my heir. They are explicitly telling me that I must marry the daughter of a Norman lord and produce a son that will eventually inherit the Dukedom of Normandy.

'The past few days have therefore been an extremely difficult time for me and have caused much heartache. To try an resolve matters I have been to Fécamp to talk with both Archbishop Robert and the Bishop of Bayeux in exile. They accept that as I have now come of age I am now longer under guardian control and am free to make my own decisions, although they hope I would still consult with them. That at least is progress.

'The bigger problem, mistress Herleva, is how to give you and William a position of status and security. You have been so dear to me and given me two beautiful children, but as I have already told you, I am not in any position of being able to marry you. The Bishops would wish me to send you away. That I cannot do. You and the children must be looked after. What I am therefore about to say to you will probably upset you greatly, but I can seen no other way forward.

'This also involves you Herluin, and I know you will be shocked and try to resist. But I really believe what I am about to tell you is in all our best interests. From my discussions with the bishops I believe they may also eventually come to agreement.

'What I am proposing my dear Herleva, is that with my consent and blessing, you should marry Herluin. I can see that you have grown fond of each other, and William loves to be with you Herluin. I can make Herluin a count – the Count of Conteville – and he will become the stepfather of our two children, William and Adelaide. I can also bequeath him some additional lands and you will both have some noble status in Normandy.

'You can continue to live in Falaise castle if you wish, or move to Herluin's home castle in Mortain. William will grow-up to eventually inherit the Count of Conteville title. He is still too young to understand what's happening at the moment and will just know that he spends even more time with Herluin. I will still see you all regularly and will be able to watch my son, William, grow into adulthood. What say you both to my proposals?'

It was long into the day and early evening before all three of them had come to any kind of agreement, and not before many refusals from them both, much crying from Herleva, and many questions from Herluin, although it was probably much easier for him to agree as he had undoubtedly fallen in love with her many months before.

Finally, Robert explained that he would go back to the bishops with proposals that Herleva and Herluin should be married as soon as possible and arrangements put in hand. If the bishops agreed, he would do as Herleva had wished and free the bishops from their exile so that the sacraments could be undertaken once more throughout Normandy.

***

The following morning Duke Robert and Herleva both attended morning prayers in the chapel, giving them another chance to talk once again about the discussions that had taken place – and for Herleva to plead with him once more about the marriage proposal.

'There is no change Herleva. My mind is made up. I will ride to Fécamp tomorrow and have further talks with the Bishops. If they agree to the proposals

I have made and discussed with you, then we will no longer be together and you will soon marry Herluin. I wish there was any other way, but there is nothing that will give you and the children security for the future. Herluin will take care of you all. I believe he already loves you as much as I do.

As this is likely to be our last day together, perhaps you would ride out with me to where we first met by the stream. That is how I would like to most remember you. I know you have learnt to ride well, so we can journey together. How say you?'

'That would be most pleasing for me as well sire. When would you wish to leave?'

'Early this afternoon after dinner. I will ask the groom to prepare the horses.'

***

Three hours later, Duke Robert and Herleva set out on their ride, passing together through the castle gates, down the hilly streets and out into the countryside, finally arriving at the place where they had first spoken on the riverbank by the stream. The sun reflecting on the water as it had been that first time several years before.

'Let's put the horses to water, while we sit on the bank to rest before the journey back to the castle. We can talk about our time together and our hopes for the future.

With the horses safely watered and grazing

quietly, they talked and laughed happily, away from any worries about their children, Falaise or Normandy. After some time, the Duke said. 'We must soon return to the castle and say our goodbyes. But I couldn't have left you free to marry Herluin without returning here. From that very first moment I saw you stepping unclothed out of the stream I had always wanted to make love to you. Now that memory will be gone forever.'

In that case sire, you shall have your memories brought back one more time.' With that, Herleva slowly took off her clothing and, standing naked with the rippling stream glinting in the sunlight behind her, quietly said 'Then let us make love right here in the long grass, and with the sun shining, as never before. I want our memories of this last day together to remain until we die.'

***

Two months later the Count of Conteville and Herleva de Falaise were married in a small family ceremony in the chapel at Falaise castle. Duke Robert and Herleva's parents and brothers were present. It meant that the Duke's young children, William and Adelaide, now had a secure future with a stepfather that loved both them and their mother – and they would still see their father from time to time.

Chapter V

1033

It was now almost two years since Herluim and Herleva, now using the title of Lady Herleva Fulbert of Falaise, had been married. Although it had been a rather difficult arrangement at first, it didn't take too long before she had returned his undoubted love and affection for her. It was a different kind of love to that with Robert. That had been an exciting teenage passion full of energy and urgency.

With Herluin it was a much more tender and gentler kind of love. More sensual and longer lasting. Herluin liked to look at, explore and caress her body. She enjoyed learning new ways of making love, of ways to please each other They could spend more time – children allowing – in each others company. It undoubtedly helped that she had long been fond of him and he was well liked by the two children. It had meant that all four of them had settled in well together, sharing their time between the castle at Falaise and relaxing at his home seat of Mortain.

Although Mortain was a relatively small Normandy village in the northwest of France (but southwest of Falaise), Herleva enjoyed her time there. It was quiet and generally peaceful, unlike the bustle of Falaise, and there were a number of other small towns quite close by that she should could visit, such as Saint Barthélemy. Herluin had not only previously taught her to ride even better than her outings with Duke Robert, but also how to defend herself if necessary. This enable the two of them to often ride out in some confidence together, and meet and talk with villagers on the way.

Duke Robert had also gone to the trouble of asking his armourer to make a small child-size sword that young William could play with, albeit not sharpened so that he couldn't cause any harm to, either himself or anyone he might be playing with. Both Robert when he visited, and Herluin, liked to make playful engagement with William in mock battles.

Wherever possible for them, one or more of Herleva's brothers would come to stay with her and the children and she was thankful that young William and Adelaide would grow up to know their uncles, as well as their aunt Beatrice. They could also meet regularly with Herleva's parents when they travelled and stayed in Falaise. That closeness that she had always had with her own family would now be able to continue.

It was perhaps not unsurprising in this happy and

loving environment that little more than ten months after their marriage, Herleva had born a son to Herliun. In acknowledgement of what Robert had done for Herliun, and the status that she had now acquired, they named their son Robert – eventually to become Count Robert of Mortain. A stepbrother for William and Adelaide. With little more than a few years in age between them, William and Robert were growing up close to each other, just as if they were real brothers, rather than half brothers. The countryside around their castle chateau in Mortain was ideal for this growing support and friendship for each other. Something that Herleva hoped would always continue as they grew up to adulthood.

Not only had Herleva had a second son, undoubtedly conceived not long after their marriage and while they were staying at Mortain, she was also now with child once again and was expecting to give birth before the end of the year. Would this be another son, or perhaps a second daughter? Either would suit her, although Herluin wanted another son.

Duke Robert, as he had promised, came to see her – sometimes in Mortain and others at Falaise – and the, by now, three children whenever he was able, which was not that often. He was also pleased that the couple were once again expecting another child. He believed it would be another stepbrother for William.

During his visits to Herleva, Duke Robert told her that much still had to be resolved with the Archbishop and Bishops to re-establish and normalize acceptance and the sacraments within the church, and he was still having problems with ongoing raids by his cousin, Alan III, Duke of Brittany into the west and northwest of Normandy.

Brittany, he explained to her, was an important cultural region to the west of France, bordering the English Channel to the north and Normandy to the northeast – the region where Alan and Robert were both laying claim to certain areas. Neither cousin wanted to give way to the other and, until the various claims could be settled, the problems would continue.

While Herleva was able to give a sympathetic ear to the Duke's feud with Alan, she again said that she felt that the best opportunity would be some kind of reconciliation drawn up between them, perhaps by their mutual uncle, the Archbishop of Rouen. The Duke promised to consider this approach, although he was still unhappy with his uncle as well, with no lifting as yet of the excommunication imposed several years before.

***

Although everything seemed well with Herleva, she now received news while at Mortain, that Fulbert de Falaise, her father and Duke Robert's chamberlain for the past few years, had fallen ill and died at the age of 53. Arrangements had to be made for his funeral and who would attend. The Duke

wanted to be present, as well as her mother Doda –
now called Doda de Falaise de Scotland – and her
sister Beatrice, while two of her brothers, Reynald
and Walter, who had been away with Robert during
his battles and travels, had to return to the castle for
the proceedings and internment.

Her brother Osbern she learnt, had been taken
ill and was on his sickbed and would be unable to
be with the other members of the family. Herleva,
Herluin and the children then made the journey back
to Falaise from Mortain to put everything in hand.

From slightly further afield, senior members of
Fulbert's small fortified chateau (castle) at Croy in
the Picardy region, which had been given to Fulbert
by the Duke, also travelled to the funeral. Herleva's
children – Fulbert was William's grandfather –
were still rather too young to be present and were
therefore looked after by a maid.

After prayers in the castle chapel, Fulbert's
body was escorted by the family, friends and a few
soldiers, to his resting place in a graveyard close
to his home. It was also explained to William that
his grandfather had gone to heaven and would no
longer see him most days. It was quite a sad time
for Herleva, but the support and love that Herluin
was able to provide at this time enabled them all to
overcome the difficult days.

***

It was a little later in the year that Herleva was able to hear better news, that the Archbishop of Rouen and Duke Robert I had finally came to a final mutual and acceptable understanding between them. His uncle, Archbishop Robert, then lifted the interdict and excommunication. In return, Duke Robert restored the Archbishop to his see, gave him back the Countship of Evereux, and returned all the Archbishop's properties that had been confiscated.

Duke Robert also returned all the property that he or his vassals had taken from the church, including everything that had been taken from Fécamp Abbey, originally a Benedictine abbey that had been founded for nuns way back in the 7th century. Part destroyed earlier in Viking raids and also by lightening, it had been rebuilt by the Duke, enjoyed royal protection and had authority over many church possessions in Normandy. It had become one of the foremost pilgrimage centers in the region.

With the feud between Duke Robert and the Archbishop finally settled, the Archbishop offered to mediate between Robert and Alan III, Duke of Brittany, with the aim of bringing their campaigns against each other to and end. As their mutual uncle, the Archbishop finally negotiated a peace pact between them – something that Herleva had long been advocating.

Sadly, before the end of the year, Herleva was to hear that her oldest brother, Walter, had passed away and another funeral needed to be arranged. It

now meant that both her father and brother that she
had often called upon for support and advice were
both now lost to her. It pleased her that Herluin
had proved to be so supportive to her when any
problems, difficulties or sadness had arisen.

***

At the beginning of 1034 at their home in
Mortain, Herleva was happily able to give Herluin
another child. This time, a baby girl and a stepsister
to William and Beatrice. Her name was Muriel De
Conteville. The combined family now numbered two
boys and two girls.

Such was the friendship between Robert and
Herluin that it seemed as if the children often had
two fathers. Although now happily married to
Herluin, and with two children of their own, she was
nevertheless still extremely fond of Duke Robert and
welcomed the time she could spend with him. She
wanted William to know, and look up to, his father
in the years ahead.

While in Falaise, the two of them liked to spend
time at the top of the castle, looking out over the
battlements at the lands of Normandy as Duke
Robert had often done in his earlier days. Although
now married to Herluin, the bond between Herleva
and Robert had nevertheless stayed very close.
Sometimes they would also take the young William
with them so that he could see just what the Duchy

was all about. At other times Herleva would go there with William on their own. It was a favorite place to be on a summers day, watching the birds – including the occasional buzzard circling high above – and the people bustling around below.

It was later that same year during the autumn and after much planning, that Robert and his English second cousins, Edward and Robert, who had now been in exile in Normandy for some time while planning to overthrow King Canute to regain the English throne, set out in a fleet of ships to invade England. Poor weather conditions and unfavorable winds made this virtually impossible without losing ships and men, although it did mean that King Canute, worried about the possibility of a drawn-out battle, sent messengers to Duke Robert to say that he was prepared to split his Kingdom with one of the brothers if that would ensure peace.

This had meant that, at least for some months and maybe longer term, a possible invasion of England would be postponed, probably until at least the Spring of the following year or even longer, if necessary. A winter invasion would be foolhardy.

Herleva was thankful for this respite, but perhaps becoming even more worried about what the future might bring.

Chapter VI

1035

It was after Duke Robert I had finally come
to more amicable and peaceful terms with his
uncle, now back in Rouen, together with the
Bishop of Bayeaux and with his cousin, Alan
III, during the later part of 1034, that his whole
attitude and feelings towards to the church had
begun to undergo something of a change. This
change, which Herleva had long advocated,
had certainly become noticeable to Herleva
whenever she saw him. He was going to the
chapel and praying more often, and certainly
had more interest than before in the Duchy's
religious affairs.

Not only that, he had set about restoring all the
church property that he had previously confiscated,
and was telling his chaplain and close family
members that he wanted to repent and find some
way that he could make up for his past actions and
sins against the church.

But before he did so, he made it clear that he

wanted to discuss his thoughts and possible future actions with Herleva and Herluin, as they would also be involved in what might happen to William.

Now back in Falaise, Duke Robert lost no time in bringing the two of them together in a secluded room at the castle. Leaving the children to be looked after by maids and servants, and again following on from an early breakfast and prayers in the chapel, the Duke started outlining to the two of them what he had been thinking of for some time.

'As you have long been telling me Herleva, I have finally had to make peace with the church. You were right all along and I should have listened to you before, but I was not sure of what I should do to be fully repentant. As you may have heard already, I have been thinking for some time of possibly making a pilgrimage to the Holy Lands, visit Jerusalem and the many religious sites and churches, go to the Garden of Gethsemane, follow in the footsteps of Jesus and see for myself where he was buried, but what would you perhaps suggest? In many ways you are more wise than I am. There is also our son William to think of, as well as our daughter Adelaide.'

'Such a pilgrimage would surely please the church,' said Herleva, 'and go a long way towards making amends to the bishops. I am most pleased that is what you wish to do, but its a long and possibly dangerous journey. And what did you mean when you said you were thinking of William. You wouldn't be looking to take him with you surely? He is far too young for such a long journey. In any case I couldn't allow it.'

'No, that's not was I was thinking Herleva. It can undoubtedly be a difficult and dangerous journey to Jerusalem. The Muslims are making the last part of the route into Jerusalem very difficult for Christians these days. It is possible I could be killed, or be taken ill and die, although I am not expecting that to happen. However, as I have no other son than William, what would his position be? The church has long said that he could not inherit the Normandy title from me, yet somebody has to be designated to take on the role. Besides, he is not yet eight years old. He would need guardians other than Herluin if he was to inherit. And I also have the council and Normandy lords to convince. As you know they seldom agree on anything, especially the future role of William. All of us must soon come to a mutual agreeable solution and a satisfactory conclusion.'

'I think that both Herluin and myself would support you making your Holy journey Robert. I also think that if we can we should settle William's position and future as well. I know he is young at the moment, but I believe he could eventually make a success of ruling the Normandy lands. He is being well educated, and he now has a stepbrother to support him in the future. Can you not make him your legitimate heir?'

Why not bring a small council of powerful guardians together that will guide and control his actions until he reaches his majority? Your uncle the Archbishop, your cousin Alan, Herluin of course, my brother, and maybe one or two others?' He might then be accepted. I would also guide him and make sure he is educated and brought to an adult as best as I can.'

'You're right of course, as you usually are. I will talk with all those possibly concerned as guardians and, if I can get agreement, will ask the most powerful of the Norman lords for support. I hope they would not disagree with either my wishes or with the church.'

***

It took several weeks for Duke Robert to finally get agreement from the church and the lords of Normandy – much to the initial surprise of all the noble followers who had all assembled at Fécamp castle – and, although it was not total wholehearted support, it was enough to have William, his albeit illegitimate son, endorsed as the future Duke of Normandy should anything happen to Duke Robert on his pilgrimage. He also ensured that this was all set out in written documents which the lords and church seniors all eventually endorsed.

The guardians were now in place and had sworn to him that they would protect and care for his young son if he did not return. Finally, he then set about planning his route, his supporting staff and enough loyal soldiers to accompany and protect them, before being ready to set off on the long and somewhat difficult journey through many different lands to Jerusalem and back. A journey that was expected to take several months to complete.

Before setting out from France in the early Spring, Duke Robert obtained letters from the Archbishop of Rouen and a number of senior Bishops, which introduced him, and his travelling companions, as church supported pilgrims to The Holy Land. With these letters it would become possible to ask for rest and refuge for a day or more from the monks and nuns at suitable monasteries and religious properties along parts of the route. Where refuge was not possible it was necessary to carry tents and sufficient quantities of food and drink − as well as various currencies to purchase supplies as they passed through different countries.

His journey to Jerusalem would see him travelling across France, through Switzerland, Germany, Austria and Hungary − travelling at times through the more favored route that would take them through the Danube river basin, with the route then going on through Slovakia, Bulgaria and into Turkey and eventually arriving at the city of Constantinople. Here, The Duke's entourage would need to obtain permission so that he and his retinue could continue on to Muslim-controlled lands and in to Jerusalem.

As part of the permission process in Turkey he would also need to pay a pilgrim tax, so sufficient monies for this also needed to be carried − something which groups of robbers along the route also knew. For this possibility they had to carefully plan a course of action on how best to defend themselves.

The aim, after travelling close to perhaps 3,000 miles, would be to finally arrive in Jerusalem and to spend a number of days there visiting the Holy sights and seeing where Jesus had spent the last week leading up to his death. This would also be a time for prayer, meeting with senior Christian leaders, other pilgrimages from across Europe, before finally recouping for the long journey back to France.

***

Before leaving on this long and arduous journey, the Duke asked to again meet with Herleva and their two children. William, now coming up to eight years old, was undoubtedly old enough to be told about his father's journey, and possibly his sister Adelaide as well. Although Herleva's children through her marriage with Herluin were still very small, they might also understand that he would be travelling for a while and would not see them. It wouldn't be an easy meeting.

***

The following morning, again after breakfast and prayers, Duke Robert, Herleva, Herluin and the children all gathered together in his private chambers to listen to what he was about to say.

'I will shortly be setting off on my journey to the Holy Lands. You will be able to follow my journey on the maps that have been prepared, and I expect to be able to send letters to you through other travellers that are returning across Europe and, William, I will expect you to send me letters that can be passed on to me during the long journey we are undertaking.

'The journey to Jerusalem and back is expected to take three or four months; longer if we have difficulties with robbers or the Muslim rulers of Jerusalem. I expect to return safely but, as you now know, I have made arrangements for you, William, to be my legitimate successor if anything does go wrong. You now have signed documents to this effect.

'William will have church and noble guardians to guide and support him until he comes of age, and you my dear Herleva and friend Herluin, will be his day-to-day parents and mentors throughout this period. I know you will honour my memory with him and show him the love, patience and understanding that I will no longer be there to give.

'I love all of you and look forward to being with you all again on my return. God bless you. Please ensure that you pray for me each day. I expect to see you once more in a few months time.'

***

It was just a few days later that Robert, his soldiers, servants, chaplain, cooks and various other personnel set of from Falaise with all the necessary supplies, clothing, tents, gifts and money to smooth the journey, as well as messages for religious leaders, monasteries and various dignitaries or relatives that they would meet along the way. It would be a slow, but steady journey across Europe, into Turkey and then through to Nazareth, Bethlehem and Jerusalem.

Much of the journey, particularly through Europe, was quite uneventful until they eventually reached Constantinople. The Muslim leaders that controlled the final stages to Jerusalem proved difficult and were demanding ever more money for a safe journey through their lands, but eventually Duke Robert made it the Holy City to follow the last days of Jesus so many years before.

**

At last, after more than two weeks in Jerusalem, it was time to prepare and plan their travels back through Turkey and on to Europe and, finally, back home to France. For Duke Robert I it would still be some months before he would be able to see his son William, daughter Adelaide, and Herleva and Count Herluin. He had missed them all.

Little did he know that while he had been away, Herleva had given birth to another daughter, a

stepsister to William and Adelaide and a sister
to Robert, who they had named Muriel – or to
give her the full name, Muriel de Conteville. The
Conteville family continued to grow. They hadn't
mentioned to Robert that Herleva was expecting
another child before he had left on his journey, so it
would be something of surprise to him on his return.

***

It was while he was on the return journey through
Turkey and Greece, and planning for a stay in the
wealthy and cultured fortified ancient Greek city of
Nicaea to stock up with further supplies, that Duke
Robert was taken seriously ill. For the remainder of
his journey in to Nicaea the Duke was carried on a
litter born by negro bearers. Arriving in Nicaea, he
eventually passed away there on the 2nd July 1035.
Too far to consider bringing his body back to France,
he was buried in the city.

Messengers were urgently dispatched to Falaise
with the news that the Duke had died and that his
illegitimate son with Herleva, William, and now at
just eight years of age, had succeeded him as the
new Duke of Normandy. Not something that Herleva
would have wished on her son at so young and age.
It would be difficult times ahead for her and for
William.

It was left to Herleva and Herluin to tell the young
William the difficult news that his father had died on

his return journey and would not be coming back. Much upset, he nevertheless understood that his life would start to be very difficult from now on.

To add to the grief, Herleva was also soon to learn that her brother Walter, who was one of William's favorite uncles, had also died while on a journey of his own to visit the Duke of Bourbon in Moulins, central France. It was a difficult and sad time for her. Walter would have been one of William's guardians if he had still lived. Now this was gone as well.

Chapter VII

1037

Two years on from Duke Robert I's death in Greece, and the more unruly of the Norman barons had further plunged Normandy into an ongoing region of major conflict in Europe. Disputes, which were frequently quite acrimonious, were common, while violence. anarchy and corruption were all rife as the Normandy barons began, or continued, fighting with each other.

Despite all their promises of allegiance to the young William that they had given to Duke Robert before his travels to the Holy Land, they were nevertheless vying or arguing with each other on who should really be taking control of Normandy, who should be the new selected guardians of the infant Duke William, or what they could capture or take of each other's territories.

This, in turn, all lead to further conflict with William's remaining guardians, particularly in the church hierarchy, and made for extremely difficult times for Herleva and Herluin who were trying to shield William from such pressures. Normandy was supposedly being ruled by a council of church and aristocratic Norman elders during William's youth, but they were elders that some of the more headstrong or youthful nobles were not ready or willing to accept. Even some of the elders were querying who should really be their leader.

It hadn't helped that Herleva was also now having to look after another, increasingly active, young son who had be born some 18 months previously; another stepbrother for William, who they had named Odo de Conteville. The loving relationship that had developed between Herleva and Herluin still continued and they had adoringly welcomed their new son into the family.

It was during this period of ever-growing family, and the ongoing Normandy upheaval, that the now ten years old, Duke William, his mother Herleva and stepfather Herluin, learnt that William's most senior church guardian, Archbishop Robert, had died in his fortified residence in Rouen, one of France's largest and most prosperous towns, and the chief city of Normandy.

The Archbishop had been one of, if not, the key senior figures trying to quell the, increasingly well-armed, conflicts erupting between the various nobles. Without his stabilizing support, the barons – and some senior church elders – were now engaged in actively creating reasons to create conflict and fight among themselves. News also filtered through to Herlava that some of them were believed to be plotting how they could either remove, or even kill, William and install one of their own.

Indeed, within a few months of the Archbishop's death, one of the first attempts to assassinate William took place, with a lone traitor somehow gaining access to Williams chamber while he was asleep before being apprehended and killed in a swordfight with some of William's nearby guards – but not before some of the guards had been injured, one quite badly, and one of Williams household servants being killed in the attempt.

Awaking to find someone in his chamber and approaching him with a sword was all rather frightening for the young William, and of deep concern for Herleva and Herluin. If he had not woken and shouted out he would most certainly have been killed. But what more could they do? Should they stay in the, reasonably well protected Falaise castle, or move more permanently to the less well guarded but peaceful and out-of-the-way Mortain castle, or perhaps transfer William's court to the former Archbishop's more heavily fortified residence in Rouen?

It was not just William for them to be worried about, although now as the Duke of Normandy he was the one mostly being targeted, but also Duke Robert's daughter Adelaide and their own three children – Robert, Odo and Muriel. To try and resolve these worries Herleva asked her close family, her husband Herluin, and her brothers who had been loyal followers of Duke Robert, to meet secretly with her to try and find a more secure and safer solution.

When they were altogether in one of Falaise castle's more remote rooms with only one entrance from a long, easily guarded corridor, and sure there was no-one nearby to eavesdrop, Herleva spoke. 'There has already been one well-planned and serious attempt on William's life – which could easily have succeeded – and Herluin and myself have good reason to believe there are others that are also plotting. Indeed, we have both been made aware that there already believed to be some individuals that may have been placed within the castle walls, and may even be integrated into the serving staff. There is also some talk of money being offered to anyone that is prepared to bring William's life to an end. I'm sure these attempts will continue, and may one day even be successful without great vigilance.

'I find it difficult to know who we can trust within the castle these days, other than family and a number of our close friends. Even then, money may prove to be a powerful incentive to somebody to get to William. But what more can we put in place?'

'There are people that can be trusted Herleva. Reynald, Osbern and myself are your brothers. You know we would do anything for you to keep our cousin safe. There is also Uncle Walter's son. We all entered the service of Duke Robert at the same time, trained with him, and travelled and fought with him in battle. He was good to all of us, as he was to you, Herluin and to our father.

'We have discussed the matter already before coming here, and have all agreed that we will stand together as personal guards to William, and aim to be with him, or close by, at all times. We are all skilled enough in swordsmanship to defeat most that might attempt to attack or kill William. As for our cousins Robert and Odo, they are not Duke Robert's sons, and should be safe, but of course we will also look out for them as well.'

'Thank you dear brothers. I could not wish for more from you. Let's hope these terrible times are soon over and we can all live happier lives, but I fear that this may be some time away.'

'William is now ten years old, quite strong and active' added Herluin, 'and I think we should now begin his own daily training in swordsmanship and fighting, and perhaps equally importantly, in how to defend himself should he be attacked. At least he will have a better chance of surviving if he can be active in warding off any villains. It will also help if we are to one-day see him become a great leader.

'The fact that castle personnel will seen him regularly training with us, and that he is beginning to have some skills in swordsmanship, should also help to deter further attempts on his life.'

At that point Herleva added. 'Herluin, you have already taught me much about being able to defend myself if attacked. Now I would like you to also help me gain some further ability with a sword, albeit a smaller one than you would use. I can keep it hidden in my chamber, but easily accessible if needed. Hopefully I would not have to use it, but I can at least be prepared.'

Following on from the family discussions, William's uncles were now regularly ensuring that they were always close to their nephew whenever possible, and all of them, including Herluin, had become involved in his day-to-day training in how to defend himself if attacked. This all meant that he was soon to be quite confident with a sword, although probably not able to yet fight off a strong assault on his own, even if he was becoming increasingly confident. It was therefore still not time to relax the strong vigilance that William had been placed under.

Herleva also made sure of that, listening intently to any gossip circulating within the castle walls and amongst the servants about possible dissent, or references to Duke William that might be casually mentioned, especially between the ladies that visited the chambers, and of course keeping a careful watch on any newcomers that suddenly appeared in the castle or its grounds. Anything that she regarded as suspicious or worrying was passed to her brothers to investigate further.

***

Sadly for the family their ongoing vigilance was soon proved to have been necessary. Happier times were definitely not to be seen any time soon. Feuding and anarchy in Normandy continued throughout the year, with further attempts made on William's life. The worst of these being while William was in a castle school room being educated. His teacher that day, and two soldiers on guard fairly close by who had heard shouting and screaming, were themselves killed, although William was fortunately unharmed as loyal guards came to his rescue and quickly whisked him away to safety.

Already the young William, Duke of Normandy, had managed to survive two very serious, and almost successful, attempts to kidnap or kill him. Would there be more?

Herleva de Falaise

Chapter VIII

1042

The past few years since plans had been put in hand to try and keep Duke William protected and safe had been little easier for either William or stress-free for Herleva and her sons with Herluin, Robert and Odo, as well as her daughter Muriel – and now also a further daughter, born in 1039, that they had named Emma de Conteville.

More years had passed and there was still much conflict and division in Normandy. Herleva was well aware that some of the Norman barons continued to find themselves unable to accept the illegitimate son of Duke Robert I as their leader and were furthering their protests, trying to rally others together to seize the Dukedom, or plot to find a way to kill Duke William.

Further attempts continued to be made on William's life with more of his guards and protectors being injured or killed in the attempts. Fortunately, with all the family and the most loyal of his followers still looking out for him and trying to ensure his safety, all these attempts had so far failed. However, Normandy had continued to be in quite a period of severe anarchy and turmoil, and was in a state of almost complete disorder.

Making matters far worse for Herleva during this challenging period was the difficult to comprehend and deeply saddening news that her brother, Osbern, had been murdered in yet another planned plot on William's life. Herleva and Herluin had felt it would be safer if William was discretely moved to his uncles more out-of-the-way chateau in the country, but one of his enemies had obviously been made aware of this and had made plans to abduct and kill the young Duke William. He was fortunate to have been able to get away, but Osbern was overwhelmed, badly injured, and died shortly afterwards.

Osbern had been appointed Steward of Normandy by Duke Robert I, retaining this position long after the Duke had died in Greece. He was therefore the most senior person so far killed in the various attempts on William's life.

Perhaps more importantly for Herleva, he had been one of those appointed by Duke Robert to be one of the legal protectors and guardians of William. Without his family support, she would have an even more demanding and important role to play in William's future. She would have to stand up to, and hold fast when necessary, when dealing with other guardians, churchmen and nobles, who all seemed more interested in promoting and enhancing their own positions, rather than necessarily supporting William.

The fact that Osbern had been married to Emma, a daughter of Count Robert of Ivry − inheriting a large property in central Normandy from her − and was a half brother of Duke Robert I, didn't help either. With ever diminishing close family support it became important for Herleva to seek other possible opportunities and solutions to best protect the young William, who was now 15 years old.

This wasn't proving easy, as William was growing in confidence and taking ever more interest in both church and political affairs in Normandy − and even wider afield with Normans having by now also conquered and taken over and were governing some lands in Southern Italy and parts of Sicily. This all lead to William becoming increasingly determined to make his own decisions in Normandy, rather like his father had done so many years before.

This wasn't going to be easy either, as justice in Normandy was supposedly exercised judicially in most cases by the Duke within the Duchy, yet in some places offences such as attacks on houses, seizures, rape and arson, came under the jurisdiction of individual barons or even a particular abbot or monastery. Not unnaturally, these barons and abbots were not keen to relinquish any of their jurisdiction or other powers, which William believed should be diminished.

Another key challenge, was that gaining

increasing power over the church and Duchy needed to be financed. This required many sources of income – with revenue coming from the Duke's own lands and forests, from his many grain mills, from coastal and river fishing rights, from salvaging wrecks and treasure-trove, from various tolls, markets and fairs, fines from justice, as well as receipts coming in from feudal dues.

Having spent much time in her younger days prior to moving into Falaise castle helping her father to keep accounts and prepare his ledgers, Herleva tried as best as she could – or was allowed to – to follow and advise William on the administration of the Duchy's estates.

Managing the Duchy more efficiently, in turn, demanded more bookkeepers, more time to implement the increasingly efficient means of collection and enforcement, as well as the maintenance of local law, and order through local viscomtes (non-hereditary nobles of rank with a role as administrators or as judiciary), local officers and public officials.

This all lead to increased disquiet and dissent among William's enemies in Normandy, and even going beyond France and into England, Italy and other countries. William was by now quite commonly being referred to as 'William the Bastard,' perhaps partly due to his unmarried mistress mother and his subsequent illegitimate birth, but also to his claims for additional powers, as well as his battlefield and often quite ruthless military prowess.

Calling him names because she had been Duke Robert's mistress made Herleva both angry and even more determined to fight his corner for him. It was not his fault that he had such parentage. It had been a coming together of two people who loved each other. There should be no need to be ashamed or apologize for that.

***

Perhaps slightly easing his, and Herleva's, problems, was some good news received regarding William's second cousins Edward and Alfred, who had spent something well over 20 years in exile in Normandy with close ties with both William, his father Duke Robert, and his uncle and grandfather. Edward had also spent time with his sister Godgifu, who was married to Drogo of Mantes, Count of Vexin in Normandy. and was also supported by some of the Norman abbots. The news that both of the cousins had finally been able to return to England the previous year meant that William believed that he now had at least some support from across the Channel.

Not only that, but before leaving Normandy, Edward had again promised that if he became King of England one day, and if he did not marry and have children of his own, he would designate William as his successor. What William didn't know at the time was that Edward had also promised the throne to three other contenders.

Nevertheless, their close relationship with William lead to English nobles travelling from time to time to Normandy to stay with William and the Norman Court, and promising to support each other in any future troubles. Making that known in Normandy certainly helped William in gaining better control over the wayward barons in the region – much to Herleva's relief.

Little more than six months after Edward had returned to England, he succeeded Cnut (Canute) the Great's eldest son Harthacnut (who had previously been King of Denmark), as King of England, in June 1041, with his coronation set for the following April and to take place in Winchester Cathedral. He was supported in his succession and rule by Earl Godwin, the most powerful of the English Earls at that time.

King Edward's Norman sympathies were soon influencing some of his early decisions, with him initiating the building of Romanesque architecture styled churches and castles, much like those in Normandy, in England – featuring the traditional and well-proven massive thick outer walls, the rounded arches, lots of pillars and large towers – and initiating the design and planning of Westminster Cathedral in London.

Although Edward had been crowned King of

England, Herleva was worried that Godwin was becoming ever more powerful, especially with Edward marrying Godwin's daughter, Edith of Wessex, in the January of 1045. She was crowned Queen of England. Edith's brother Harold Godwinson, together with Edith's Danish cousin Beorn, were then given earldoms in southern England (Harold becoming Earl of East Anglia) – making Godwin's family the major rulers in the whole of southern England.

Such developments lead Herleva to start thinking about the role that William might have should Edward die without a successor. The Possibility of William eventually becoming King of England seemed to be becoming more remote. Would, or could, Edward still regard William as his heir as King? Would Edward and Edith have any children to succeed as king? And would the powerful Godwin family ever accept William as King of England anyway?

While all this was of some concern to Herleva, it was the ongoing regular challenges to Duke William's authority that continued to plague the Duchy. The older members of the nobility and church tended to resent William's authority over them, while the younger members felt he was someone they could outwit or defeat if it came to a battle.

This all meant that Herleva constantly urged William to have his loyal followers and their cavalry and foot soldiers well trained and prepared in every element of archery, swordsmanship, and the use of lances. Whenever possible she would like to watch them undergoing such training. It was not that she new much about preparing for battle, but that she liked to feel reassured that they would be ready should the time come – whether this was planned or unexpectedly forced upon them.

Sadly, three of William's guardians were in the end violently murdered during William's early and teenage years, as well as one of his tutors. It was undoubtedly Herleva, together with her own close family, and some specially chosen loyal followers that she had brought together, which meant that she had so far managed to protect William through a quite long and difficult, challenging and formative period of Normandy history. A challenging period that was unlikely to have come to an end.

What Herleva's guidance and protection had done was to give William more purpose in trying wherever possible to stamp out anything that he regarded as misrule, anarchy, lawlessness, or as being unchristian. His earlier years of recklessness, it seemed, were – under Herleva's ever-watchful eyes and thoughtful advice – now much more under control.

Chapter IX

1047

It had now been two years since Herleva's daughter with Herluin, William's younger stepsister, Adelaide, had married Enguerrand II of Ponthieu when she was just fifteen years of age. The same age that Herleva had been when she first met Duke Robert. Such an age to get married was not unusual for the nobility at this time. Indeed the marriages were often arranged by their families to ensure suitable lineage and, hopefully, good fertility so that healthy heirs would be forthcoming.

Adelaide had undoubtedly grown to become a very attractive and petite teenage girl, much like Herleva had been when Robert had spied on her in the stream. It was little wonder that there were Norman nobles looking to marry her. As for Enguerrand, he was the son of Hugh II, Count of Ponthieu, and would eventually succeed his father as the Count (in 1052), so could be considered quite a catch.

Unfortunately the marriage was then later annulled by the church after a few years, partly due to her brother, Duke William, being illegitimate. In such circumstances therefore, Adelaide was deemed of unsuitable lineage. However, Adelaide retained and continued to live quite well in Aumale, a Normandy region in the Seine-Maritime department, which had been given to her on marriage by her brother William

It was also now two years since William's second cousin, King Edward of England, had been married to Harold Godwin's daughter, Edith of Essex. This had been the cause of some celebration amongst those that knew him from his years in exile in Normandy, although if the couple did have an heir (the marriage did not produce any children and Edith was eventually sent to a nunnery, probably because she was childless and Edward hoped to divorce her) then William would not have any chance of succeeding to the English throne. But that was the least of William or Herleva's concerns at this time.

By the autumn of the previous year there had been rumours of further plotting to replace William as the Duke of Normandy, especially by one of his cousins, Guy of Burgundy. Hoping to placate Guy, William gave him castles in Vernon and Brionne. This had the effect of achieving very little, for Guy decided that as he now had a powerful base he should then set about trying to overturn and rule the Duchy himself.

This had meant that the past few months had once more become an extremely difficult period in Normandy, both for William, and probably even more of a worry for his mother Herleva. It had been a period when some of the enemy barons, led now by Guy of Burgundy, and some of William's own more disgruntled viscounts, had been able to ambush him as he journeyed the marshy terrain that lead from Valognes, a fortified stronghold of Norman dukes based in the Cotentin Peninsula, in the northwest region of Normandy

Although the ambush was ultimately unsuccessful, William was nevertheless able to find out, most likely through torture, from some unfortunate prisoners that had been taken, that the barons of Cotentin and Bessin, together with several others nobles, had apparently been conspiring to kill him for some time, and were believed to be in the process of raising a strong rebel army to fight against him – and ultimately take over the rule of Normandy.

Following his successful escape from the ambush, William travelled quickly back to the safety of his own fortified castle at Falaise to talk with his loyal followers and with his family. Although he was now 18 and leading an army, he still liked to refer and talk with his mother when difficulties in Normandy arose. She was much more impartial than the church or war lords.

'I have received news that Nigel of Cotentin, Rannulf of the Bessin, Guy of Burgandy, Ralf

Tesson, and some others are between them planning to raise an army of as many as 25,000 men to attack Falaise castle with the aim of killing me and becoming the new rulers of Normandy.' explained William to Herleva. 'On my own I can probably raise an army of little more than 5,000 men and would be unable to withstand an attack from an army of that size, but what more can I do?'

'It is little more than five years since you gave shelter in Normandy to King Henry of France,' said Herleva 'and then provided military support to him during his successful quest to regain his kingdom from his mother and younger brother. Indeed the King knighted you for your loyal service at that time.

'Even long before that, your father had also provided loyal support to the King. There are probably no more loyal and faithful supporters in the whole of France to King Henry than our own family. Why do you not immediately ride to his court in Poissy to remind him of this support? An attack on one of the King's most faithful supporters is almost an attack on the King himself. Surely he would support you in a battle with the rebel barons? Talk with your brothers. They would need to be putting our own army together and preparing them for battle while you make the journey to Paris and back.'

The following day, after long discussions with stepbrothers Robert and Odo, with Herluin, some of his cousins, and other senior members of his court, William was ready to set-out with an armed escort on the 150 mile or so ride to Paris and a meeting with King Henry to seek his support.

***

It was well into the summer of 1047 before William had fully brought together and fully prepared an army of supporters, still numbering little more than 5,000 men – albeit very well-armed, trained and disciplined – while King Henry had raised an army of his own of around 10,000 and was ready to march towards Caen – the main base of the much bigger rebel army – in Normandy and join with William to fight with the rebel barons and their forces.

Before setting out, William gathered his brothers, his cousins, Herluin and Herleva together in Falaise castle to outline the military strategy that had been agreed with the King. This was to have cavalry on each side of their own line of foot soldiers and specialist bowmen, who would then in position to lead cavalry charges, both into and around the enemy lines to try and break them up and cause confusion, and so win the battle.

The other key element of the family getting together was to agree a way forward if William and/or either of his brothers were killed during the fighting. 'Who was to take over as the next Duke of

Normandy? 'The battle we are shortly to undertake may take just a few days, or could possibly last into a week or more.' explained William. 'There will undoubtedly be deaths on both side, but if we succeed the main troubles should come to an end.

'Should I be one of those killed I would propose that my eldest stepbrother, Robert, becomes successor as Duke of Normandy and, after Robert, should he also be killed, then Odo would be the next Duke. Hopefully we can all agree?' Without any dissent to either the battle plans or succession?

William then turned to his mother. 'We will look to send a messenger each day to keep you informed mother of our battle progress. Hopefully it will always be good news. Should anything happen to any of use you know what steps to take. Where we would like to buried, and who is to become the next ruler of Normandy.'

'I will pray for you all each day, for you to win your battle, keep you safe, and to see you all back at Falaise sometime soon. God bless you my sons.'

***

A few days later, and now with both sides encamped around Caen, the final preparations for battle the following day were being set-out to the supporting nobles by the leaders of both armies; William and King Henry briefing the combined royal army, and saying final prayers before retiring for the night.

The following morning, again after prayers, battle commenced. Although widely outnumbered, King Henry and William were buoyed when one of the rebel barons, a large Normandy landowner, Ralf de la Roche-Tesson, decided to change allegiance and, instead of attacking the King's army, he joined them on the first day of the skirmish and rode with his 120 knights to attack the rear flank of the rebels, causing much surprise and some confusion amongst them. With no result at the end of the first day, both sides withdrew for a night's rest, but not before William had despatched a messenger to his mother in Falaise and held meetings with the King and all their senior knights.

It was the next day when the real battle between the two sides began in earnest on the plain at Val-es-Dunes, close to Count Herluin's home town of Conteville. Far better organized and lead, the disciplined and stronger royal army and their cavalry soon caused the rebel army to break apart and, leaderless and panicking, to largely flee west towards the Orne River, pursued by both the cavalry and foot soldiers of King Henry and William Duke of Normandy.

In flight and steadily being run down, it was a pretty bloody battle for the enemy. Thousands of the rebel soldiers were brutally slaughtered while fleeing, while many others were pursued and driven into the waters of the River Orne, drowning in numbers in their heavy armoury while trying to cross to safe ground on the other side, leaving multiple bodies – both dead and the severely injured and dying – floating away downstream.

Although it very much a one way fight despite the number that had been arraigned against them, not all the rebels were able to be defeated on the day by the armies of Duke Robert and the King. Guy of Burgundy managed to escape and flee with most of his followers to the east and, holed up in his castle stronghold at Brionne (ironically previously given to him by William), continued to hold out against the combined might of the royal army, Nevertheless, the bulk of this major rebellion was successfully quashed, with William and his brothers all safely able to return to Falaise and to their mother.

Finally, together with the support of King Henry, the backing of the church and most of the Normandy nobles, Duke William at last began to establish his authority, and some level of peace, over the duchy of Normandy – but not before William (following Herleva's encouragement and support) had been forced to pardon many of the barons, counts, and other nobles that opposed him and had even tried to kill him. But they did now have to swear allegiance to him.

Even then, with Guy of Burgundy still resisting at his fortified castle in Brionne (the one given to him by William), it would be several more years before all of Normandy would be under the full control of William, and it would be some five years or so before he had to face another revolt.

***

For Herleva, it was now a period when she had time to think of the family, her three sons and the daughters of both Duke William and Herluin, and perhaps of her own future. It was once more time to talk with William, Robert, Odo and Herluin.

All together again at Falaise, Herleva began to set out her thoughts on the next few years to come. 'We now finally have some level of peace in Normandy. It's surely time we began to think of a suitable wife for you to marry William. There must be a woman amongst the nobility that you would like to raise children with to continue the dukedom in the coming years. It's important to all of us. And is Falaise the best place to establish a more powerful and secure base? You should start looking at all these possibilities.

'Odo, you trained as a cleric and I think you are probably more suited to be a senior churchman in the longer term. Is there a place in Normandy where you might wish to be the bishop – one day archbishop, like Duke Robert's uncle? Maybe build and establish a new cathedral. Little work has taken place on repairing or building churches during all the troubles in the past ten or fifteen years. It needs a strong church leader to set a building and repair programme in place. And Robert, we also need to find a wife for you to continue your own line of family succession.

'Together, we have grown to become a strong and close-knit family in which we have all successfully supported and protected each other. Let's make sure we can stay that way, in turn being recorded in history as the most respected ruling family in Norman history.

'For Herluin and myself, we are slowly getting older now. One day we are going to need a place to be buried, a peaceful resting place where, hopefully, we can be finally laid together. Perhaps all of us eventually in the same place, or at least close to each other, and maybe your wives and children as well. Can we not find and create a small peaceful abbey and gardens in Normandy as a suitable memorial place for us to be remembered in the years to come? Maybe somewhere near the sea or a river, not too far from Falaise, Caen or Conteville.

There is much for you to think about, but I believe now is the time for us all to work together, see if we can create a long lasting peace and prosperity for Normandy and to look to all of our futures.'

Chapter X

1050

Now three years on from the battle in Val-es-Dunes and the subsequent family gathering in Falaise and much had changed. William, Duke of Normandy, had finally proposed marriage the previous year – to his cousin Matilda of Flanders. She was the second daughter of Count Baldwin V of Flanders, one of the most powerful counts in France, and King Robert II of France's daughter, Adela of France. A most worthy marriage.

Apart from having the King of France as her father, Matilda was also a descendant of King Alfred the Great, whose daughter Aelfyhryth had earlier married Balwin II of Flanders. He was nicknamed Baldwin the Bald after his maternal grandfather, Emperor Charles the Bald.

With historical family ties to England, it was not unexpected that Baldwin V would maintain close link with that country, often giving refuge and support in the form of armed guards and entertainment to English exiles, such as the dowager queen Emma of England while she was exiled in Brugges.

Being related to the King of France and to Alfred the Great, meant that William and Matilda's proposed marriage would not start without various challenges. Matilda's father, Count Baldwin, was not pleased about the prospect of them marrying, believing that with her much stronger royal heritage she could do much better than marry an illegitimate duke. Furthermore, Pope Leo IX had even gone so far as to refuse to let them get married as he believed it would be an incestuous relationship, possibly because they were second cousins, or otherwise related through a daughter of Duke Robert II.

Despite these setbacks, William and Matilda decided they would plan to get married anyway, even without the Pope's approval, but supported and encouraged by Herleva and William's two stepbrothers, Robert and Odo. All of them prior to the proposed wedding had met with Matilda's father, Count Baldwin of Flanders, and had lengthy discussions on the subject before he would agree to the marriage. The aim of the discussions had been to persuade him of the benefits of the union.

'My grandfather and father, the former Dukes of Normandy and, more recently my son, William, have long provided military and personal support to Flanders.' explained Hereleva. 'It is region of great importance to both of us. Trade from England and the northern countries comes through Flanders into Normandy and down into southern France, Portugal and Spain, while trade comes back through Normandy and Flanders. We are interdependent on each other. We have long supported each other in battle. A marriage between our two families will further cement these ties.

'Although William was born out of marriage, he has since distinguished himself in battle and was knighted by none other than your wife's father, King Robert of France. He has a legitimate title now, and has proven himself in battle. It has also been determined that he is in line to possibly become the King of England. Your own family has descendants from King Alfred of England. Surely William must be worthy of marrying your daughter?'

'You're correct of course Herleva,' Baldwin accepted. 'we are both closely connected in trade and commerce, between France and England, and also across France, as well as historically in keeping Scandinavian intruders at bay. If the King of France is prepared to support William in both battle and in love, how can I object?'

Thanks you Lord Baldwin. Let's put together a grand wedding. Perhaps the King will attend, and most of the faithful Normandy knights, the senior bishops who might be prepared to defy the Pope, and all of our extended families. It would help to extend the peace that has been achieved, and unite the duchy further.'

Baldwin would probably have agreed to the

marriage in the end anyway. He had been in
rebellion against Henry III and needed some
powerful support from within France. William
already had a good reputation as a fearless soldier
and even amongst his rivals was well respected. To
have William as an allay was a carefully thought out
strategy.

William's successes in battle, his support from
the King of France, and his proposed wedding to
Matilda of Flanders – albeit still not formally
approved by the Pope – now enabled him to finally
start dominating both the Norman aristocracy with
both his political and military power, and through
the church. He also had a powerful ally in his father-
in-law in the neighbouring county of Flanders, and
he had ambitions to expand into Maine and thereby
strengthen Normandy's southern borders. This
dominance in Normandy and beyond enabled him to
appoint his key supporters as viscomtes, bishops and
abbots in the Norman church and as administrators,
further cementing his controlling position.

Finally, Herleva believed she had achieved her
wish for William to be married. Perhaps she would
now live to see some or all of the children that the
marriage would hopfeully produce, and maybe
Robert and Odo's children as well.

By supporting his proposed marriage to Matilda,
and given his new found dominance in Normandy,
William was able to reward his step brother Odo
de Conteville by appointing him to the Bishopship

of Bayeux, even though he was still only around
16 years of age. Construction of a Cathedral at
Bayeux had originally commenced as far back as the
Roman period, but Odo was tasked by William with
continuing its building and making it in to one of
the leading centres of Normandy worship. Between
them, Odo and William encouraged foreign church
leaders, monks and leading scholars from across
Europe to visit Normandy and, in particular, the
growing religious centre of Bayeaux.

***

Unfortunately the planned marriage between
William and Matilda did not actually take place at
this time, or at least become formally recognized,
until some time later. Pope Leo IX had continued
to forbid the wedding. An actual wedding date was
never recorded but it is believed to be somewhere
between 1050 and 1051. The Pope however, ended-
up being imprisoned just a few years later.

It was also during the intervening years following
the battle at Val-es-Dunes that Herleva and
Herluin, with the backing and support, as principal
benefactor, of their son Robert and the church
leaders, commenced the building of a small abbey at
Grestain, near the town of Fatouville. The town was
around four miles from the pretty harbour town of
Honfleur on the southern bank of the estuary of the
Seine, just across from le Havre and very close to

the exit today of the Pont de Normandie. The Abbey Notre Dame de Grestain was finally consecrated in the spring of 1050.

Much to Herleva's delight, William and Matilda seemed to be very happy and loving together – and soon becoming a fruitful relationship. Although probably not yet formally married by now, it was nevertheless only later in this year that William was able to visit his mother while she was staying with Herluin in Mortain, and tell his mother that his 'wife' Matilda was pregnant and was expected to give birth to their first child early the following year.

'I'm so pleased for you both.' Herleva said when they were all together. 'You will make excellent parents and I look forward to meeting your first child. If it is boy he will have to start learning his future responsibilities from an early stage, and I can tell him much about the family's history.'

***

It was little more than two months later that Herluin sent a desperate messenger to William, Robert and Odo to say that their mother, Herleva, had been taken quite ill at home in Mortain, with the family doctor saying that he was concerned that she might be in danger of not recovering. He asked them to urgently travel to his castle at Mortain and see their mother for, possibly, the last time.

Within the week, with Herluin, William, Robert

and Odo, as well as the daughters of Duke Robert I and Herluin by her side, Lady Herleva Fulbert of Falaise, fell into a deep coma and passed peacefully away in her sleep. Much loved by them all, she had provided a firm but much needed secure and stable grounding in Normandy life and responsibilities to all of her children. She had established a position of power and influence in the Duchy that few in the future would come close to achieving again.

As requested, Herleva was laid to rest in the well-tended and peaceful grounds of the newly built Abbey of Grestain. The same Abbey that later her husband Herluin, her eldest son Robert de Mortain and his wife Mathilde de Montgomerie, were all also to be interred in.

***

So brings the life of Lady Herleva Fulbert de Falaise, mother of the illegitimate Duke William of Normandy, and his stepbrothers Odo, Bishop of Bayeaux and Robert, Count of Mortain, to an end – although it was far from the end of her legacy to the ruling houses of Europe, to the English crown, and even to the church.

Although it's argued that she had no royal blood herself and is often painted as a 'commoner' or simply a 'tanners daughter', she did appear to have historic Viking noble connections. She certainly didn't marry into royalty herself, although her son,

William, did become King of England, as did two of her grandchildren, William Rufus and Henry, while one of her daughters with William was to become betrothed to Alphonso IV, King of Spain.

William, together with Herleva's sons with Herluin, Odo and Robert, William's stepbrothers, between them went on to become the dominant and wealthiest landowners in England following the Conquest, while William is often cited as undoubtedly one of, if not the greatest, soldier and ruler during the Middle Ages – both in France and in England.

Not a bad legacy for a tanners daughter to leave.

The Sequel

Within a few months of William's mother passing away, and sadly before Herleva had any chance to see him in the early months of 1051, William's pregnant 'wife,' Matilda of Flanders, gave birth to a son, known as Robert Curthose, who was to later succeed William as Duke of Normandy after his father's death in 1087. Disappointedly, he was to prove a somewhat incompetent administrator and ruler of the Duchy and, although he made attempts to seize the English crown from his brother, was unsuccessful.

Much has been written about William and his conquest of Harold at the battle of Hastings, his subsequent coronation as King of England, and his rule throughout the country, but not always that much about the role his stepbrothers Odo and Robert from the marriage of Herluin and Herleva, played in the battle, or the role of some of Herleva's family members.

At the battle of Hastings, Odo commanded some 3,000 mounted knights – the first time cavalry had ever been used in England – and was said to have been instrumental in King Harold being defeated, while Robert was also a key figure in William's army, as was William de Falais, Herleva's cousin.

Sadly, William and Matilda's second son, Richard of Normandy, who was born in 1054, died in a hunting accident in the New Forest in 1074. Their third son, William 'Rufus' (because of his red hair) succeeded his father as King William II in 1087. He was said to be addicted to all kinds of vice (including sodomy) and died – possibly murdered – while hunting in the New Forest in 1100. He had not married and had no heir to succeed him.

Following the death of William II, William and Matilda's fourth son, Henry, who had been born in Yorkshire, claimed the throne as King Henry I of England. Under Henry, England moved to a much more bureaucratic country, introducing central and local administrators, accountancy recording and an exchequer to manage the country. He ruled the country until his death in 1135, leaving no heir.

His nephew, Stephen, then took the throne from Henry's daughter – who had initially claimed the throne – and ruled England until 1154. His reign in England was marked by a great deal of anarchy, as well as a civil war with his cousin and rival, the Empress Matilda, whose son, Henry II, was to eventually succeeded Stephen.

William and Herleva's daughter, Muriel de Conteville, went on to marry William de Massey, and gave birth to just one child while staying at Dunham Massey in Cheshire. She died in the year 1076 in St Edmunds, Suffolk, England.

Herleva's brother, Reynald, known as Lord Reynald de Falaise, Lord of Croy, Nord-Pas-de-Calais, Picardy, died at the age of 51.

Following his mother's untimely death and after the birth of their first child, William had finally decided to move his residence from Falaise castle to Caen, as his mother had proposed some years before, starting the ongoing development – followed by his sons William II and Henry I of England – of the castle and towers built there over the next forty, fifty or more years.

Built on a rocky outcrop overlooking the Orme valley, the castle, enclosed by stone walls spread over five hectares, was able to control all the surrounding access routes, eventually becoming one of the largest medieval enclosures in the whole of Europe – a leading European royal stronghold where he and subsequent Dukes of Normandy and Kings of England would gather for major political and military meetings. It dominated the town of Caen first founded by his grandfather Richard II, Herleva's father-in-law.

William and Matilda were to eventually have nine children, four sons and five daughters – most of them born (apart from Henry) before William set out on his Conquest of England – and every monarch of England since then has been his direct descendant. As William's mother, Herleva de Falaise can also be said to be directly descended to every English monarch since the Norman Conquest.

Of William's daughters – Herleva's grandaughters – the eldest was Cecilia of Normandy, and she was to become a significant figure in Normandy as the Abbess of Saint-Trinité at Caen, a Benedictine monastery for nuns that had been founded by William in 1062. Cecilia died in 1126. It was in this monastery that William's wife, Matilda, was herself finally laid to rest in 1083.

Matilda had largely governed the Duchy of Normandy in William's absence In England and had only joined him after a year so before retuning to Normandy for much of the rest of her life, while William mainly ruled in his new Kingdom across the Channel. He only returned to Normandy in the latter years of his life.

Their daughter Adela, married Stephen, Count of Blois. One of her children was to become the Bishop of Winchester, while another, Stephen, became King of England in 1135 and died in 1154.

The most gifted of William's daughters and Matilda's favourite, was Constance of Normandy, the second born of his daughters in 1057. She was a Princess of England by birth and, through a forced marriage with Alan IV, Duke of Brittany, became the Duchess of Brittany. Said to be an able administrator, but unpopular, she died in 1090, and it is said that her husband arranged for their servants to poison her.

As for Herluin, Herleva's husband, he soon married another woman, Fredesendis, after Herleva's death. It was a woman that he already apparently knew, as she was listed as one of the benefactors of Grestain Abbey where Herleva was buried. Herluin and his new wife Fredesendis went on to have two sons: Raoul de Conteville, who later held land in Somerset and Devon, and Jean de Conteville, who died at an early age.

It is too easy to say that Herleva's main claim to fame is that she was simply the mistress of a Norman Duke, husband of a Count, and mother to a King. Nevertheless, it is a historical fact that nearly 1,000 years since she became the Duke's mistress, her genes have extended through to a great many of the European ruling families and monarchs of today.

Despite all this historical heritage, her own story has largely been unknown and unwritten, mainly living on through the story of her sons, William, Odo and Robert, who can be said to have changed the course of both English and French history following the battle of Hastings, and then continued through her grandchildren.

Her three surviving sons between them, were to become the largest landowners in England at this time. William became the King of England. Odo, his stepbrother, became Earl of Kent, acquired vast estates in southern England and served as regent of England when William was absent, while his stepbrother Robert, was one of the Conqueror's main supporters in the invasion of England and the second largest landholder. Within 20 years he owned over

800 manors with land from Sussex to Yorkshire in the North and Cornwall in the west.

William de Falais, Herelava's cousin, was also given lands in England – holding 17 manors in Devon as tenant-in-chief of the King – and later married the daughter of Serlo de Burcy (a major landowner in Somerset, England), while William's daughter, Emma de Falais, later married William de Courcy in Somerset around 1094. Both Serlo and William were from families in the Calvados region of Normandy.

Under the rule in England of William Duke of Normandy and his stepbrothers, the Norman aristocracy effectively took over most of the governance of England, replacing English Earls, landholders, administrators and bishops with skilled Norman administrators, and embarking on a major programme of building castles, grand halls and churches.

Indeed, it is estimated that something like 500 castles were constructed over the 20 years following the Conquest, including Norwich castle, Colchester castle (begun 1066), Dover castle, Rochester castle and Warwick castle (built 1068). Building of the Tower of London was started soon after William's coronation and included stone shipped over from Normandy. Today, some 90 of these Norman castles are still standing. From this base, England undoubtedly became one of the most powerful governments in the whole of Europe.

It is perhaps also interesting to note that Grestain Abbey, which had been founded by Herleva and her husband, Herluin, and where she was buried, was to become a focal point after the Conquest in the Normans being able to predominately take control of the church of England; a period when a great many new priories and churches were built across the English counties. Indeed, many of the churches identified in the Domesday book actually mention Grestain as their founding church, while the Abbots of Grestain were to ordain many of the new English priests.

Consolidating his rule, William put in place a survey of England, creating the Domesday Book, which today is one of the country's oldest legal documents. Many new words, both Latin and French, were added to the English language throughout his time as King, as well as the foundation of today's system of bureaucratic government.

The Normans also successfully established the harvesting of grapes in Southern England on land in which both soil and climatic conditions were particular suitable for the growing of grapes, with the Domesday book recording that there were over 40 vineyards in the region.

It has frequently been written that William was illiterate and was never able to speak English. This seems difficult to comprehend. Herleva's father was a successful businessman in Falaise and she was initially working in the business, recording and writing transactions and preparing other records. She was undoubtedly reasonably well educated before entering castle life.

It is also known that William was being educated and had tutors in the castle during his early years. At least one of his tutors is recorded as having been killed defending him. As a teenager and already governing the Duchy he would have been responsible for reading and signing documents. He was seen as a fair and an intelligent and able administrator. As for speaking English, Herleva's mother – who he would often see and spend time with – was born and grew up in Scotland before marrying and moving to Falaise. He had English second cousins that were exiled in Normandy and at times living at the castle in Falaise, and one of their sisters married into Norman nobility. King Edward and Earl Godwin also travelled from England to stay, meet and talk with William.

So how did the story of Herleva's sons, William, Odo and Robert, come to an end?

William ruled England until his death, on September 9, 1087, although most of the last 15 years of his reign were spent back in Normandy, in Rouen. He died in Italy after falling from his horse while bringing his father's body back from Nicaea Cathedral where he had been buried. Robert was then re-interred in Italy, while William's body was brought back to Normandy and buried in Rouen.

His stepbrother, Odo de Conteville, Bishop
of Bayeux and Earl of Kent, served as regent of
England whenever William was absent. He later
tried to rebel against William and was imprisoned,
only to be released by William while on his
deathbed. Odo later joined the first of the Crusades,
but died in 1097 while he was travelling to Palermo
on route to Jerusalem, where he was buried in the
Cathedral.

Robert de Conteville, who was made Earl of
Cornwall by William after Hastings, married
Mathilda of Montgomery, Countess of Cornwall and,
although he lived much of his time in Normandy
he died in Cornwall in 1090. His body was then
returned to Normandy, where he was buried in
Grestain Abbey, close to his parents Herleva and
Herluin who were already buried there.

Apart from her son who had become King
William I, two of Herleva's grandchildren, William
II and Henry I went on themselves becoming Kings
of England.

As for Herluin, Herleva's husband and the father
of Odo and Robert, he died in 1072 at his castle in
Mortain, Normandy, and is buried at the Abbey of
Grestain, which he had founded with his first wife,
Herleva, and their son Robert.

Herleva was undoubtedly quite an extraordinary
woman. She had a significant influence on her sons
and daughters, and what they were to become in
life, gained power within Normandy, and ultimately

had an impact on the long-term historical future of France, England and much of Europe.

About the Author

Michael Fairley has written or contributed to more than 20 technical, historical and biographical books in a career which has extended through education, research, training, magazine publishing and exhibitions. He has additionally been a major contributor or author of five international encyclopedias, and a regular speaker, chairman or moderator at conferences, summits and seminars on a global basis.

Other biographical and historical titles written by him during the past ten years are:

Born to Soldier

Two Thousand Years of Kentish History

The History of Labels

One of Life's Great Charmers – A biography of Charles Kay, Olympic gold medallist and variety artist

William Kay – Cotton manufacturer and liberal benefactor